CORGI CRISIS

A SMALL TOWN COZY MYSTERY

MOLLY MAPLE

MARY E. TWOMEY, LLC

UNTITLED

Corgi Crisis
Book Two in the Apple Blossom Bay Series

By

Molly Maple

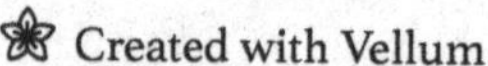 Created with Vellum

To Mallory Crowe,

Who came into my life and looked at my mess as if I wasn't beyond repair.

I really hope you're right.

When Hannah Hart goes to the grocery store in the small town where she lives with her eccentric aunt, the last thing she expects to find is a dead body.

Hannah is certain someone had to have witnessed the crime; it's only a matter of getting them to talk. But when the fingers begin to point in her direction, she knows she needs to watch her back.

With her sweet toy Pomeranian by her side, Hannah takes in a curious corgi, who saw more details to the murder than any human might catch. Hannah knows that if she doesn't get to the bottom of who murdered Hank, the small-town killer will strike again.

"Corgi Crisis" is an inclusive cozy mystery, filled with layered clues and quirky moments, written by Molly Maple, which is a pen name for a USA Today bestselling author.

THE CREEPY BACKROOM

Waking up to my sweet toy Pomeranian laying her head on my stomach is just about the best feeling in the world. Though Cricket is six years old, her squat stature, curious nature and fluffy hair make her look like she is still a pup.

Though my Aunt Em's ranch-style home isn't set directly on the beach, with my window open, I can feel the ocean air wafting in through the gap.

If there is a town, a home, a life more perfect than this, I do not know it.

I sit up slowly and kiss Cricket on her wet nose, letting her listen to my plans for the day while I take my time stroking her thick fur. I can't decide if it's more red, brown, or gold today. Either way, she shines with happiness as I rub the velvet of her ear.

"Today is the day," I tell Cricket, who licks my face over and over.

My gosh, being kissed just for waking up? How did I go my entire life without a dog? While I wish the manner in which she came to me didn't involve her previous owner passing away, I am grateful fate trusts that I will care for this sweet dog.

"Today I'm going to the grocery store to apply for a job." I nuzzle my pup's nose with my own. "Is it a management position? No, it's not." I cup her small face with my left hand. "Is it using my business degree? No, it's not. But let me tell you, I can't imagine I will be stressed out stocking shelves at a grocery store. Aunt Em said I should find something that's good for me. I don't know if stocking shelves is it, but it'll give me a little income while I figure out what it is I'd like to do."

I'm not applying because I think the work will be simple; I think this will be good for me because it's not a job that turns my stomach.

After graduation, I was supposed to go straight into a career using my business degree, but I just couldn't do it. Compliant my whole life to the point of letting my parents pick my degree, I didn't realize how ill-suited I was for my impending profession until I was supposed to go job hunting in my field, and I just couldn't do it.

I ended up working at a gas station for a handful of years, much to the embarrassment of my parents, who constantly remind me that I should do more, have more, be more.

So, my parents sent me to the beachy town of Apple Blossom Bay "to take care of Aunt Em" they promised. Though, when I got here last month, it became clear that my spontaneous and often unconventional aunt needs no help from me whatsoever.

I stand from the spacious queen-sized bed and select my most responsible, no-nonsense ensemble—black pants and a white blouse with black shoes. Can't go wrong. This is my least wrinkly blouse, too, which has to count for something.

I tug my messy strawberry blonde curls into a ponytail, and figure I look as good as I should for a job interview. I straighten my posture, claiming every bit of my five-foot-eleven inches.

Cricket doesn't leave my side, even as I flit through the hallway to the kitchen, where Aunt Em is fiddling with the burner on her purple stove. "Good morning!" she sings to me.

I inhale a deep drag of the spring ocean air that is now combined with the smell of bacon. "Any morning with bacon in it is a good one to me." I sneak a piece off the paper towels, my eyes rolling back as the flavor awakens my palate. "Remind me why I lived anywhere other than with you?"

Aunt Em chortles at the compliment. "Let's chalk it up

to insanity." She is wearing a flowing silk dress with no waistline, dotted with large pink orchids on the long sleeves. She looks like a spring fae with her shoulder-length straight black hair swept back from her angular jaw and high cheekbones. She stands two inches taller than me and wears her superior height with the confidence of a supermodel. "Did you sleep okay?" she asks me as she plates a few pieces of bacon, a slice of toast and a fried egg for me.

"I slept great. How do I look?"

"Like you're ready to get any job you go after." She narrows one hazel eye at me in a faux scold. "Though, I told you that you don't have to work, you know. You just moved here last month. You haven't taken barely any time to live and figure out what it is that makes you come alive. I don't want you committing to something that makes you miserable."

Cricket yips twice, taking umbrage with that assessment, as if she is not the creature who has brought color to my cheeks and a pep in my step. As if a job can even compare with the joy she brings me.

I feed her a piece of bacon after filling her dog bowl and getting her clean water, all while mulling over my aunt's words. "I'm okay with acclimating slowly to life in Apple Blossom Bay, but I can work a job while I figure out what makes me come alive. What if the thing that makes me come alive is stealing yachts? I might need to have bail money stashed away, just in case."

Aunt Em laughs at what is clearly the furthest thing

from what I might ever do with my life. I am a rule follower through and through. But sure, in my imaginary life, perhaps I steal boats and race across the coast.

Aunt Em sits with me, her upper lip curling when I take a bite of my toast. "Um, you forgot to put butter on that."

I shrug. "It's fine dry." And that's exactly what it is. *Fine.*

My aunt blanches, though I'm not sure if her revulsion is from the dry toast or from the F-word that slipped off my tongue. "Fine? You woke up today, deciding life would be nothing more than 'fine'?" She shakes her head at my inadequate priorities. "That toast needs butter, jam or both."

I smirk at her insistence over things that I'm not sure matter all that much. "I think we're out of the jam Phyllis made. Butter might be nice."

"That's more like it. I don't want you to live like a vagrant." She shakes her head. "Dry toast. I never. It's like I've had no influence on you whatsoever."

I love her insistence over the things that never mattered to me before. Aunt Em is big into the details that make life a luxury, even if they are as insignificant as a pat of butter.

We chat while we eat, which was never the case in my house growing up with my parents. My dad read the paper while my mom scrolled on her phone.

Aunt Em is a treat to eat breakfast beside. She tells me all about the planting she is going to attempt this week, and the family she is taking to look at houses in hopes of selling them the abode of their dreams.

After I kiss her cheek and ready myself to head out the door, I promise Aunt Em that I'll pick up a jar of jam when I'm at the store for my interview.

"Do it, and Phyllis will slap the jar out of your hand. If she comes over and sees store-bought jam in my fridge? I'll never hear the end of it."

I snicker at the mental image of the woman in her seventies growing violent over traitor jam.

I hate leaving Cricket behind, but I'm guessing that's not exactly the move of a professional vying for a job if I take my dog with me on the interview. Though, I'll admit, I am decidedly less confident as I drive down the flower-lined streets in my red sedan toward the grocery store without Cricket by my side.

All through college, I let my introverted nature take over. I don't like to use the term "shut-in," but it might apply in broad strokes. The moment Cricket came into my life, I started to appreciate the fresh air of the great outdoors. The spring weather breathes new life into my bones, reminding me that it's okay I am not a finished product.

"I can do this," I say aloud to myself in my visor mirror as I check to make sure I look professional enough for the interview.

My shoulders sink as I take in my reflection.

I look like a hapless twenty-five-year-old blah. Not a

woman. Not a proud bisexual woman. Not a happy dog-owning woman. A "blah" with frizzy strawberry blonde hair that should be curly, and too many freckles across my nose to count. Why would they hire me? I don't have experience stocking shelves. I ran a cash register at the gas station. I have little frame of reference for what any other job might entail.

Plus, I was born without my right hand. Sometimes people regard me as if I can't do things that people with two hands can do. I don't want the owner of the store to see me as a liability, or worse, a charity case.

The grocery store is open, with a dozen or so customers milling about. The carts are lined up near the entrance, and the woman in her fifties with brightly dyed blonde hair at the cash register waves at me with a big smile.

Because she recognizes me.

Because I live here.

I move toward Betty with what I hope is a smile, but I'm sure my nerves are making me look like I am fending off a grimace. "Morning, Betty. I'm here to meet with Larry for an interview."

She claps for me as if I have already secured the position. Her slender frame bobs up and down excitedly. "That's fantastic, Hannah! Em just texted to let me know you were on your way. She said to tell you you're a shoo-in." She waves me toward the rear of the store. "Larry's in the backroom. Go on through the doors."

My smile turns to a grimace because the interview is minutes away from happening. "Thanks."

Why am I nervous? This isn't my dream job. It's not something that defines whether or not I am a useful person.

Still, my palm is sweating as I head to the back of the store, meandering near the meat section because I am unsure which of the backdoors Larry might be behind. There is also a set of doors to my left, so I'm not totally sure where I should be headed.

I don't just want to walk through, since I see two sets of doors along the back wall. And I'm not an employee, so going into the "Employees Only" area seems like an obvious violation of the rules.

Still, Betty directed me here, so after I look from side to side to make sure no one sees me trespassing, I go into the door at the end of the meat section, hoping this is the correct one.

I tiptoe through the cavernous space. It has flickering lights that make me have to squint so I don't get a headache. The rest of the store meant for customers is well-lit, but this seems to be straight from a horror movie, complete with an echoey quality to my steps and a lingering cold that chills my spine. "Hello?" The cheery bright walls of the grocery store are gone now, replaced with concrete from floor to tall ceiling. I shiver as I crane my neck to see if there is any hint of a person nearby who might direct me to Larry.

I chew on my lower lip as I walk further into the wide back area, which is lined with rows and rows of inventory.

I really do love putting things in order. Maybe it won't be the most thrilling job for me to stock shelves, but I enjoy it when items are all aligned.

"Hello? I'm looking for Larry," I call to absolutely no one. My voice sounds timid and there's an A/C unit bellowing to drown out anything short of a shout.

I know this is a small town, but I expect someone to be working back here somewhere.

When I hear a whine, my footsteps pick up, moving me toward the sound. As I go nearer, I notice a tinge of distress, so I trot instead of walk. "Larry?" I call again into the cold, gaping backroom.

When I maneuver around one of the tall shelves stacked with pallets of breakfast cereal, a motion near the ground catches my eye. Though the light is terribly dim as it flickers, I make out what is certainly a dog, whining over a lumpy blanket on the concrete floor.

"Oh, pup! Are you lost?" Though, as I approach the squat corgi, a thrill occurs to me. "Do they allow dogs back here?" I kneel so I can run my fingers over the dog's short caramel-colored fur. Instead of keeping my thoughts to myself, I speak to the dog, who seems in need of a friend. "If I got a job here, would they let me bring Cricket?" Glee lights up my face at the prospect. That would be a dream come true. With my dog by my side, I don't reach for anxiety as often as I normally might. She calms me down and breaks the ice with strangers.

My insides lift with my next inhale—a deep breath that tells me my happiness is buried in that very idea.

The corgi leans into my touch, licking my wrist to let me know she is friendly.

"What are you doing back here all by yourself?" I kiss the top of the corgi's head. "Did someone drop a package, and you're cleaning it up for them? I hope you got to eat something tasty." I pick up the blanket beside her, which has something bumpy underneath.

The corgi whines and then lets out a mournful howl when the blue blanket slips over the secret it was hiding.

I gasp and leap backwards, crying out in terror. My voice echoes through the concrete walls, making it sound like there are several of me calling out for help.

I back up, my eyes fixed on the horror as my mouth refuses to close. I drop the blanket several feet from the gruesome sight, though I probably should have covered it back up for propriety's sake.

The corgi sticks by my ankles, whining because neither of us knows what to do with the dead body of a man, lying abandoned in this cold and lonely space.

2

A LITTLE BIT OF HONEY

If my heart ever slows from its mile a minute pace, I will be surprised. I am still clutching the stale coffee that was pressed into my palm after Larry came running to the sound of my screams. My eyes are wide; I'm not sure I've blinked. I sit in the breakroom of the grocery store holding my coffee, sipping occasionally just to keep myself from screaming when the sight of the body comes back to my mind over and over again.

"You sure you didn't see anyone near the body? No sign of who could have done this?" asks Deputy Hanson, who is sitting at the round table across from me. Sure, the break-room is well-lit, almost to make a point that you will not fall asleep on the job in here. The rest of the backroom was dim, lit only by flickering bare bulbs overhead like some grotesque nightmare.

I shake my head at Deputy Hanson, taking in every

detail. The red hair he has in the front is spiked with a little too much product. His mustachioed face is serious as he studies me with his brown eyes. "No one was back there. I called around for anyone, but it was just me and the dog."

The poor corgi hasn't left my feet. She looks to be full-grown, well groomed, and in need of a little comfort. I am now not ashamed of my afternoons spent wanting a dog so badly that I would watch dog shows. I even went so far as to research more about the various breeds in my spare time. This corgi is longer than Cricket and certainly stockier, but I still get the feeling that I could pick her up for a good lap snuggle.

Or maybe I just want to hold her to comfort myself.

Betty rings her hands as she paces through the breakroom. "I'm sorry, Larry. I sent Hannah to the back, but I didn't tell her where to meet you. She went through the inventory door, I'm guessing, instead of to your office." She shakes her head at herself. "Like that's the thing to care about right now. Hank is dead!"

I don't know Hank, though that's no great surprise. I have only been living in Apple Blossom Bay for a few weeks, so there's a great many locals I have yet to meet. "You knew him?" I ask Betty.

She nods her head, dabbing at the edge of her red nose with a brittle napkin. "Of course. It's Hank!"

I have no frame of reference for his name, but I don't remind her of that obvious fact.

Deputy Hanson jots something in his notebook. "The body looks to have been there for quite some time. Either that, or Hank was murdered somewhere else, and then his body was dumped here. Stabbed, by the looks of it."

Betty sobs loudly into her napkin at the deputy's crass words. "Poor Hank!"

Larry leans his butt on the counter, his arms crossed. His deep-set eyes are hollowed out with grief. "I just went fishing with Hank last week. He was talking about taking his boat out at night to see if there would be fewer tourists. He was hoping to get a little quality time with the fish." He lowers his chin, his brushed-back dark brown hair falling over his forehead. "I guess he won't be taking the boat out now."

Larry and I haven't been properly introduced, not really. He doesn't look my way, other than to refill my coffee when I reach the end of my cup. He looks to be in his early fifties, with tight shoulders and a jerky manner to his movements. It's like he's used to carrying stress, though today, it's far more than even he was prepared to bear.

Deputy Hanson taps the end of his pen to his tiny notebook. "How is it that the new girl found the body when she doesn't even work here? Who else is on the schedule?"

Larry scratches his shaved cheek. "I had to let Wally go last week, so it's just me and Betty this week. Truthfully, Hank could have been in that aisle for quite some time with no one finding him. I'm a bit swamped. I haven't had time to restock the way I normally like it done." He motions to me. "That's why I was glad to see this one's application. We could use the help, being shorthanded like this."

I perk up marginally. "You'd still like me to interview for the job?"

Larry's head tilts to the side. "After finding Hank the way you did? If you still want to work here, the job is yours."

"Thank you. I can start tomorrow." I can't even feel the elation of having secured the job. The image of Hank's lifeless body still haunts my mind.

So, I do what comes naturally and pet the dog at my feet, willing her sweet nature to calm me. She's got deep, soulful eyes that contain a sadness so acute; I cannot stop my hand from petting her. "Who does this sweet lovebug belong to? I think she's been traumatized enough for one day."

Larry clears his throat, pausing a beat as he gets choked up. "That's Honey. She belongs to Hank." It's when he says those words that his eyes tear up. "She's been with him for ten years. He takes her out on the boat whenever he goes fishing. She never leaves his side, really. Hank even baked her a birthday cake and had a celebration with a few of us he goes fishing with on the regular."

Deputy Hanson leans toward me. "It's important I get any details you have on this, Hannah. Anything at all might help."

I feel awful because I have nothing that can't be obviously ascertained by anyone who examines the body. I reach down and pet the corgi every few seconds. I know she feels the stress in the room that is nowhere near cresting. "I didn't get a good look at the details. I never met Hank."

Deputy Hanson's eyes fix on me, a hint of accusation brimming in the brown. "Well, his dog sure seems to know you."

I bristle, suddenly finding my spine as I sit up straight. "Are you implying something?"

Deputy Hanson motions to the dog who has not left my side. In fact, the second my hand leaves her, Honey's maw rests on the side of my calf, her neck craned to get closer to me. "I'm saying outright that Honey doesn't take to anyone who isn't Hank. I've known that dog from a pup, and she's never cozied up to me like that."

My mouth firms. "Maybe Honey just plain doesn't like you." I scratch behind Honey's ear because I can't help myself. "She's been through a trauma. She saw her best friend in the world dead. Who knows how long she sat by his body, waiting for help to come." I shake my head at the awful image of Honey crying by Hank's side, possibly for days on end. "What happens to Honey now?"

Deputy Hanson leans back in his seat. "I take her to the shelter. Hank didn't have close family members, but if they want her, they can take her."

Before I can stop myself, before I can ask my aunt's permission, I am already volunteering my help. "I can watch Honey until Hank's family decides what to do with her." I should probably discuss this with Cricket, too, since my sweet toy Pomeranian loves having my undivided attention.

I really need to stop doing this—seeing a dog in need and volunteering to take them in without permission or a plan.

Maybe I need to stop, but I know I can't. When I see a dog who needs a friend, my heart tugs so hard that I wonder if it was even beating in the moments before I saw the canine soul in distress.

My Aunt Em is always pushing me to do something good for myself. Adopting Cricket was the single best thing that has ever happened to me. My heart turns tender at the thought of Honey being left in a shelter without someone to snuggle her after she's just lost her daddy.

This might get complicated, but I cannot turn off my heart, no matter how irrationally it beats. I cannot let Honey go to a shelter when she's just seen her owner dead. She needs constant cuddles on the couch. She needs treats and a warm doggy bed.

Who am I kidding? She'll sleep in my bed with Cricket and me.

The mental image of that Heavenly scenario is the only thing that pushes out the gore of Hank's body. I gather Honey closer to me and fix the officer with my most pathetic pleading stare. "Please?"

It is clear that Deputy Hanson doesn't trust me, but

Honey and I mesh so well that he can hardly say no. Plus, if I take Honey in, then he doesn't have to make the trip to the shelter with a dog who might pee in his squad car.

"Oh, fine," the deputy says. "You can stop by Hank's house tonight to pick up the dog's things. But don't go too far out of town. Until we find Hank's killer, I want all three of you ready to pick up your phones when I call." He motions to Larry, Betty and me with borderline suspicion shining through.

I gulp but remind myself that I am innocent and have nothing to hide.

Betty hugs me on my way out after the deputy wraps up with his interviews that lead him precisely nowhere productive. "I promise this will be the worst day of working here. Every other day will be better than this. When things aren't so terrible, I can't wait to get to know you. Any niece of Emily's is a dear friend of mine."

I can't get over how readily people hug me here. I don't give off that snuggly vibe. I'm tall and awkward and usually not very well put together. I get nervous in new scenarios. I can't remember the last time I made friends this easily.

I guess that's the charm of a small town. Or perhaps that quality is unique to Apple Blossom Bay.

Larry shakes my hand. "Thanks for looking after Honey for Hank. That's right nice of you." He leans down to pet Honey, but pauses before making contact. Larry shows Honey his hands first, as if this sweet corgi might be prone to growling even at friends. "If you want to bring Honey into work tomorrow on your first day, I wouldn't say no to that. She's not going to be happy at home all alone. She's used to being with Hank every second of the day."

I perk up at the offer. Joy floods my system, lifting my posture and brightening my countenance. "Really? You'll let me stock shelves with Honey?"

Larry nods nonchalantly, as if he didn't just make all my dreams come true. "Sure. Why not?"

I shouldn't push my luck, but I go one further because frankly, I can't always speak up for myself, but I can sure go to bat for a dog. "Would it be okay if I brought Cricket, too?" I fiddle with the hem of my shirt, nervous that I'm asking too much too soon, and showing what a neurotic nut I sometimes am, and might always be.

Larry waves off my request that caused me a fair deal of anxiety just to voice. "Sure. The more the merrier. The kids love seeing the dogs, and everyone in town loves Cricket. The locals know not to pet Honey unless she gives the okay."

The urge to hug this man in his fifties is strong, but I resist it, bobbing happily on the balls of my feet. "Thank you. We'll see you in the morning—the three of us."

I didn't think a murder scene could turn into one of the best offers of my life, but when the sun hits my skin as I walk outside with Honey at my heels, I realize that Apple Blossom Bay just might be my favorite place on earth.

3

TWO DOGS

While I wasn't sure how Cricket would get along with Honey, I guessed correctly that my aunt would have zero problem with me bringing home another dog.

"It's only temporary," I tell her, though that's what I told her about Cricket, and that fluffball is officially mine now. "Just until Hank's family decides what to do with her."

Aunt Em is still sitting on the floor of the living room with Cricket on her lap, donning her friendliest tone so as not to spook the newcomer.

Honey is crouched beside the recliner, looking warily out at Cricket and my aunt. She keeps her proximity close to me as I lean forward, resting my elbows on my knees.

My aunt hasn't gotten up since Honey and I came home, keeping her movements to a minimum. "Hannah

Grapefruit," she scolds me, using my childhood nickname that is way better than the dreaded "Hannah Banana". "You know I don't care if you bring home a hundred dogs. I told you to do something good for yourself, and I can see you took my advice. I love Honey. The thing is, Honey only loves Hank. She's never bitten anyone, but she takes time warming up to people." She motions to Honey, who is clinging to my ankles. "Though, apparently you've made your way into that very exclusive club. Odd." She tilts her head to the side, sizing up our closeness as if she's never seen Honey do anything so strange. My aunt blinks twice, then smiles. "Of course she can stay, especially now that I see how much Honey loves you. If Cricket approves, then we're good."

I move to the floor so I can pull Honey onto my lap. She is far heavier than Cricket, but somehow she fits in my arms as if she was always meant to be here. She kisses my chin, which is the green light for me to rub my cheek against hers.

That deep sigh finds me—that signal from the universe that this is what my soul has needed. This is the thing that is good for me.

My aunt holds Cricket, who is panting happily, straining her neck so she can kiss me. A faint whine sounds in her throat, letting me know that seeing me and not being able to be near me is pure torture.

While Cricket has never met a stranger, it is clear that Honey is nervous, clinging to me the way she is.

Aunt Em releases Cricket, who sniffs around Honey with her fluffy forward-curling tail wagging. I wait for a sign that my two sweet girls will be able to coexist, giving them the space to feel each other out, no matter how long the introductions take.

I let Cricket kiss me while I hold Honey like a baby in my arms. Her back legs tighten to her body, but she doesn't growl or struggle to get away from Cricket.

Then finally, Honey's hind legs loosen from her body, and she turns in my arms to reveal her belly to Cricket—the eternal sign of surrender and peace from one dog to another.

Cricket sniffs and then licks Honey's neck, winning my heart and drawing a squeal of glee from my aunt.

Quick as a shuffle of limbs, Honey sits on one of my thighs, and Cricket hops atop the other. Neither dog growls or nips. In fact, Honey leans into my shoulder with a contented sigh, as if she doesn't mind having a bigger family than just herself and Hank.

Aunt Em smiles at the three of us, her eyes wet as love beams out from her. "This is going to work. Oh, Hannah. I love how happy they are here. That's what I want my house to always be—a place where happiness lives, and where lost souls come home to find themselves. It's the Apple Blossom Bay way." She moves to Honey's other side, leaving her hand in plain view. Aunt Em waits for the corgi to grant permission before she pets the sweet dog. "I can't believe Hank is dead. Just terrible."

"I don't know much about him," I admit. "Larry mentioned he goes fishing, but that's all." My nose scrunches. "Why would Hank be in the backroom of a grocery store? Was he planning on visiting Larry at work?"

Aunt Em shrugs. "I don't know. But an empty backroom is a fantastic place to dump a body, if you ask me. Especially when the place is short-staffed."

I curl one arm around Honey and the other around Cricket, keeping my fur babies close. "Did Hank have any enemies?"

Aunt Em chuckles. "No one has enemies here. Everyone in Apple Blossom Bay gets along well enough. It's the magic of the ocean breeze," she assures me. "It does away with any resentments that might build up." She shakes her head. "Hank loved fishing. He was retired from the fishing trade, and only went back out on the water for himself—for fun. Played cards with a few of the old men around here once a month. I'm sure they won't be too thrilled to hear their pal died. They're a bunch of old men who love playing cards, fishing and little else. Larry's the young one in the group, if you can believe it."

I smirk because Larry looks to be in his fifties. "That's a nice ritual, having a regular game of cards to look forward to."

Aunt Em points to the boxed-up puzzle sitting on the coffee table. "Speaking of nice rituals, you finished that one last night. Are you planning on doing another?"

I sit up straighter, proud of the fact that it only took me

two days to do a five-hundred-piece puzzle. "Deputy Hanson told me to stop by Hank's house this evening to get Honey's things. I was going to drop off the puzzle and rent a new one on the way. Any requests?"

Aunt Em stares up at the ceiling in thought. "Something with flowers. I want nature inside my house and outside."

I love that she has her own passions. My aunt is always fiddling with her flowerbed in the backyard, making the world more beautiful with her plants.

"Deal." I pet my dogs while they take turns kissing me. I adore the cozy feeling of being encased in furry affection. "I got the job, by the way. It's just stocking shelves, but I'm looking forward to it."

Aunt Em holds up one finger. "So long as it doesn't take you away from your puzzle time with the girls."

I nod, loving how normal the whole oddity sounds. I am now living in a small town where an eccentricity like a puzzle club is a perfectly acceptable way to spend one's evening. And calling my fellow puzzlers "the girls" is a nice term for the senior citizen women I meet up with to put together massive puzzles once a week.

Because I have friends now. Friends I get to see regularly, whom I look forward to being around, and with whom I share interests.

I don't know how I got to be so lucky.

Aunt Em's phone rings, and she answers on the second chime. "Hi, Macy." Her sculpted brows push together.

"How would I know something like that? It was my niece who was there, not me. And I can't imagine they've gotten around to doling out Hank's personal property. They only just found the body this morning."

I frown at Aunt Em's end of the conversation. I kiss both dogs atop their maws because they shouldn't have to hear something so tawdry.

When Aunt Em ends the call, I quirk my eyebrow at her. "Macy sounds lovely. The body was just found like, two hours ago."

Aunt Em rolls her eyes. "I'm not even the first person she called. Apparently, I came after all the guys Hank plays poker with, his neighbor, and Deputy Hanson."

"What does Macy want?"

Aunt Em draws in a long sigh. "Hank took fantastic care of his boat. That's all he really did with his time. He loved Honey and that boat. So of course, Macy wants to know who will be getting Hank's boat."

I hold Honey tighter to my side. "She's not asking about Honey, though, right? Macy doesn't want to take her?"

Aunt Em shakes her head, a small smile casting itself onto the three of us. "No, baby. I don't think anyone has a huge heart for Honey. She shies away from anyone who isn't Hank." She motions to the snugglefest happening on the floor of her living room. "I've never seen her cuddle up to anyone who wasn't Hank. This is good, Hannah Grapefruit. Honey needs some comfort and sweetness after seeing her best friend dead."

I kiss both the dogs. "Sweetness is exactly what these two loves deserve. I'm going to get more ingredients to make another batch of dog biscuits while I'm out."

"Sounds good. I've got a few showings today, so I'll be in and out. Miss me lots?"

"Miss you heaps and lots," I assure her.

And it's true. When my mother sent me out here, it was under the guise of taking care of my aunt. Imagine my surprise when my aunt needed nothing but someone to have fun with in this gorgeous sea-soaked small town.

I stand and fix Cricket's leash on her collar while Aunt Em locates some crafting twine to use as a leash for Honey.

"Maybe you should call a friend," Aunt Em suggests. "You know how Hank got to be in the poker club?"

"How?"

"He called up a few friends and made plans. You live here now, Hannah Grapefruit. Might as well put down some roots while you're ours."

While I would have no clue who to call up if that same advice was given to me back when I lived in Chicago, now that I'm here, I know exactly who I can call to see if they want to spend the afternoon together.

I take out my phone and connect with Jada, grateful that this sweet town has not only given me two dogs to cuddle and care for, but it has also given me a friend.

4

MRS. FINCH

When Jada meets me in the parking lot of the Forgotten Stock Market, both of us are displeased to find the grocery store closed for the day.

"I don't know what I was expecting. There was a murder victim found there just this morning. Of course they would close the store to investigate," I mutter as we walk on the pavement away from the store.

The sidewalks here all sparkle because, upon closer inspection, there is golden glitter poured into the cement. It's a lovely little touch, especially when the sun is shining on this warm May afternoon.

Jada takes Cricket's leash because when she tried to take Honey's rope, Honey sat her corgi butt down on the concrete and refused to take a single step. "I needed apples. Boo." Then Jada shakes her head. "Like that's the thing to focus on. I can't believe someone killed Hank. That man wouldn't hurt a fly. Whoever did this is just awful. Like, lacking the basic ingredients of a soul kind of awful." She flips her elbow-length box braids over her shoulder, showing off the pink thread that's been woven through.

We wander in tandem on the glittery pavement while Honey and Cricket stroll through the grass. Luckily, nearly everything in this town is within walking distance, so Jada guides us toward Hank's street, which isn't even a mile from the grocery store.

When we reach the stretch of houses on the dead-end street, Jada waves to a neighbor who is out watering her flowers in the front yard. "Good afternoon, Mrs. Finch." Then to me, Jada says, "Mrs. Finch rents the house next to Hank's. She lives here during the warm months."

Instead of sending back a cheery greeting, Mrs. Finch holds the sprayer in her fist and aims it at Honey. "Get that creature away from my lawn!"

I hold up my arm, indignation pushing past my usually timid nature. "Stop! Don't point that at the dogs."

Mrs. Finch looks to be in her sixties, with most of her salt-and-pepper hair tucked under a straw hat to shield her pointy features from the sun while she gardens. "That mutt of Hank's peed on my flowers last week. Right on my flowers! Now they're wilting. I swear, if that fleabag steps one paw on my lawn, I'll hose her down to teach her a lesson." She scowls at us. "At least you have her on a leash. Hank lets her run wild."

I highly doubt that's true, but I don't say as much.

A police car pulls into the driveway of Hank's house, cutting off my tart retort before I can form one.

Jada stands beside me, chest puffed. "Honey is a corgi, not a mutt. And she just lost her best friend. Show a little respect."

Cricket yips to support Jada's indignation, because she's just that good a dog.

Mrs. Finch's upper lip curls. "Lost her best friend?"

Jada nods. "Hank was found dead this morning." She leans forward with her hand on her hip. "Know anyone who's cruel enough to spray a dog with a hose? Because that person might be on the suspect list, especially when she runs her mouth about a recently deceased man on the day his body was found!"

I gape at Jada's moxie, wearing the same look of astonishment as Mrs. Finch.

The woman sets down her hose. "Hank died?"

I nod, keeping my attitude to myself. "Any information you have on who might have done something so horrible would be helpful."

Mrs. Finch squints one eye in my direction, motioning to Honey. "What's going to happen to that mutt of his? Are you taking her to the pound?"

I stand straighter in defense of Honey. "She's staying

with me so I can look after her until Hank's family decides what they want to do."

Mrs. Finch nods, as if that makes me worthy to talk to, since I am taking away her source of frustration. "Good." She shakes her head as she picks up the hose again and squirts the bushes in the front yard. "I don't know who could have gone after Hank. He didn't have many guests, other than the guys once a month for poker." Her head tilts to the side. "Hank's too friendly. That's the problem with the lifers around here."

"Lifers?" I ask, making sure to keep both dogs on the pavement so they don't step onto her lawn.

She motions to Jada. "The people who never leave. Like the whole world is all fishing and farmer's markets. Hank's a lifer. You can tell because they walk slower, and they invite strangers into their homes all willy-nilly." She points a crooked finger at me. "Last night there was someone going door to door, selling lawncare. As if the people here are too lazy to mow their own grass. I don't open the door to people like that, but Hank let the boy into his house. Glutton for punishment, I tell you." She shakes her head. "I never."

Jada flips her dark hair over her shoulder, indignant. "I'm proud to be a lifer. Come on, Hannah. Wouldn't want Hank's death to overshadow the shine on Mrs. Finch's petunias."

Jada stomps off toward Hank's house, but I stand on

the sidewalk, sizing up the new information. "Hank let someone into his house last night?"

Mrs. Finch squints at me, making me wonder if her upper lip remains perpetually curled no matter her mood. "Yeah. What of it? Hank was too trusting, and that's probably what got him killed. See? Lifer."

My mouth pulls to the side. "Don't you think that's information the police would want to know? That lawn-care salesman might be the last person to have seen Hank alive."

Mrs. Finch throws her head back, looking up at the sky. "I swear, this is Hank getting back at me from beyond the grave for hating his dumb dog. No, we can't just let the police do their thing so I can do my thing. My flowers could die, and all people will care about is if a lifer did something stupid that got him killed. Big mystery."

I frown at Mrs. Finch, my hackles raising over anyone referring to Honey as dumb. While I didn't know Hank, I feel an affinity for him, since he loved his dog so well, and I intend to do the same for however long I get to look after Honey. "You can't possibly be this cynical, caring more about your flowers than you do a human being."

Mrs. Finch sets down the hose and tromps toward Hank's house. "Flowers don't make dumb decisions that lead to my day being interrupted."

I keep Honey tight to my heels as I walk toward Hank's home, where Jada is waiting for us on the porch. Though Apple Blossom Bay is a haven for lost souls, it seems some prefer their creature comforts over the solace this small town has to offer.

I can only hope that Mrs. Finch's love of her flowers and hatred of her neighbor didn't lead to Hank's untimely demise.

5

HONEY'S BELONGINGS

Jada has no trouble making her frustrations known to Deputy Hanson the moment we enter Hank's home. Arms akimbo, she rants to the officer, who looks ready to punch out for the day so he can escape the drama.

"She threatened to spray Honey in the face! I mean, can you imagine? This dog just lost her owner, and Mrs. Finch pulls something like that."

Cricket yips in support of Jada's indignation.

Mrs. Finch folds her arms over her chest. "Yes, imagine that. I was ready to defend my own property. The nerve."

They go back and forth, which isn't something I have interest in watching. Instead, I take Honey and let her lead me through the house. I gather up a dog bone, two chew toys that are shaped like fish, and a blanket that looks handknitted strewn atop a hair-laden dog bed.

Cricket takes her time sniffing every corner while I keep Honey by my side.

I can hear Deputy Hanson trying to be patient as he pulls information out of Mrs. Finch about the lawncare salesman who happened by the neighborhood. But all I can think is that this is the last time Honey will be in her home.

I kneel beside the corgi, who licks my face as if I am the one who is having a hard day, and not her. My arms go around her pudgy form so I can kiss her cheek to offer whatever comfort I have at my disposal. "We'll take your toys and your food, your bed and your blanket. Is there anything else you'd like to have? I know you're going to be sad tonight when you have to sleep in my house and not your own."

Honey whines on my shoulder, as if she actually does understand what I'm saying.

I'm not surprised. Dogs are more insightful than most, I've found. Or maybe it's that I communicate more freely with canines than members of my own species.

When I stand, I move to the closet and pull out a flannel shirt. "This might help, having something that smells like Hank. I'm so sorry, Honey. This is just the worst day for you." I wrap Honey in Hank's flannel, admiring the way Honey sniffs the familiar scent of her owner. She whines, as if asking me where he could possibly have gone.

This whole thing is breaking my heart.

I grimace when I locate the mostly gone bag of dog

food. "This is the expensive stuff," I mumble to Honey, taking in the price sticker on the front. "I know it's not a good idea for dogs to switch food. It can mess up their stomachs. But goodness, I'm not sure I can afford this yet." I gnaw on my lower lip, hoping my new job will help me get Honey the food she requires.

I gather up Honey's things and make my way to the front door, where Mrs. Finch is sassing the deputy for whatever reason.

Jada calls Cricket, who runs happily toward the door without a care in the world, so we can get away from the surly neighbor who values her petunias more than human life.

Mrs. Finch throws her arms up in frustration. "If there were stricter leash laws in this city, we wouldn't have that problem, would we."

Deputy Hanson sighs, not bothering to hide his annoyance. "I'm asking you about the lawn maintenance company, not whether or not Honey should be put down and buried with Hank. Do you remember anything about the person? Man? Woman? Uniform? Truck?"

Mrs. Finch looks around the quaint house with an upturned nose. "So, this is how a bachelor lives. Disgusting."

Jada calls over her shoulder on her way out the front door. "The more Mrs. Finch doesn't answer your questions, the higher up on the suspect list she goes, Deputy!"

I love how fearlessly Jada pushes for results.

Mrs. Finch harrumphs. "It was a man. A young man with nothing better to do than waste my time. He had a yellow shirt on with a stain, as if that's the way to get new customers. He had the audacity to knock on Hank's door at dinnertime. Can you imagine? In the middle of dinner!"

It took so long to get the smallest detail about the salesman that I barely care about that tangent anymore. I am more focused on Mrs. Finch, and her overt loathing of her neighbor.

If Mrs. Finch was willing to spray a sweet dog in the face with a hose, would she be the kind of person who might murder a man in cold blood?

6

HANK'S CHILDREN

Jada and I leave the house with a garbage bag of Honey's things and our two dogs in tow. Luckily, I am able to replace the twine with Honey's proper leash, which makes walking her much easier.

Jada talks a mile a minute about her students while we stroll in step back to my place. "So then Andrew blew on his soda and the foam went all over Katy's white dress. Of course. Katy's mom was upset. Though, why she would send her daughter to school in an Easter gown is beyond me. My kids play outside. They get dirty. We do experiments in class. It's not the place for perfect gowns."

I chuckle as a light breeze flits over my arms. "Well, I guess Katy's mom learned that the hard way."

Jada is a kindergarten teacher, and from what I can tell, a fantastic one at that. She's always making crafts for her students and coming up with activities that involve learning while interacting. Her energy is infectious, even while she regales me with stories of her school day.

Jada talks the entire way to my house, and by the time we get there, I feel as if I know little Katy's pain and Andrew's absentminded nature. "So, all in all, it was a regular school week. No accident reports to fill out, which is good."

I open the door to the house, stopping short when I find my aunt bent into a pretzel shape on the floor of the living room.

I balk at her. "What are you doing?"

Aunt Em exhales as she grins up at me, slowly untangling her limbs. "I was thinking of taking up yoga. The Recreation Director is doing a class by the oceanside. I'm practicing."

I help her up off the floor. "That sounds like a good way to spend a morning."

"That's what I thought. I'm taking Phyllis with me. I could sign you two up, if you like."

"I'm good." I grimace, unsure how to tell my aunt that I am not all that bendy, and I've never done yoga in my life.

Or any sports, for that matter.

Jada presses her hands together in front of her chest and bows. "Another time. I'll break out my good stretchy pants just for you."

Aunt Em fans her dewy features. "I would be honored." She fixes me with a knowing stare. "I thought while we were down there, we might be able to talk to Macy, who usually goes walking down the coast Saturday mornings. Might be able to keep her away from Hank's boat, in case she gets any ideas."

Jada gives her a knowing look. "Ah. Very smart. Is Hank's boat still in the harbor?"

Aunt Em shrugs. "No idea. But what with how quick Macy called to see if anyone knew who was getting the thing, she's a person I want to keep my eye on. We all keep tabs on her when we can."

My mouth falls open. "You think Macy killed Hank?"

Aunt Em shakes her head. "Heavens, no. I think she's going to try to snoop around his boat and see what she can take without anyone noticing."

Jada turns to me to offer an explanation. "Macy is a hoarder. Whenever someone moves or has a garage sale, she comes by the day after and tries to take whatever didn't sell." She kneels and runs her fingers over Cricket's thick fur. "I think it's quirky, but everyone who lives on her street is fed up with her hoard. If she starts snooping around Hank's belongings, it's only a matter of time before his things end up lost in her jumbled collection."

Aunt Em nods. "Whenever there's a garage sale, we take turns occupying Macy, so she doesn't bring home more things."

My heart goes out to the woman whom I'd assumed was a murder suspect, given that she inquired about

Hank's boat mere hours after his body was found. "That sounds rough."

I was assuming Macy might be the killer, instead of seeing that she might just be a collector without limits, which I cannot imagine would lead her to murder Hank.

"Phyllis is spending tomorrow with Macy, and I'm going to keep an eye on Hank's boat Saturday morning when I do yoga, so Macy doesn't let her curiosity guide her into trouble. I'm going to ask her to join me."

Though I don't know this woman, my mother's "everything in its place" attitude zips through my spine. Only, my mother would be appalled at Macy's mess, whereas I desperately want a project.

I love organizing things. I can't wait to start working inventory tomorrow to let myself go crazy with organization on a massive scale.

But today is about Honey—making her feel welcome and introducing her to her new temporary home. "The Forgotten Stock Market was closed, so I couldn't get any ingredients to make treats for Honey and Cricket."

Aunt Em waves me toward the kitchen. "Then let's give them the old tried and true reward for a dog."

I follow her with the two dogs at my heels. "You got any ideas?"

"Any dog is happy as long as I can open a jar of peanut butter."

I snicker at my aunt, who makes a show of "whipping up" two spoons of peanut butter.

"I have a million cookie cutters in my classroom I can bring by the next time you make dog biscuits," Jada chimes in, clapping her hands excitedly. "Finally, they'll get used for more than just making play-dough shapes."

"We can make a batch now. It just won't be exactly what I had in mind." I frown thinking of the missing key ingredients I wanted to procure to make dog biscuits for Honey and Cricket. Instead of fresh ginger, I opt for the dried stuff, which I'm sure will be just fine.

Jada motions to the dogs, who are happily slurping peanut butter off their spoons. "I'm not sure these two are all that particular."

Aunt Em pours herself a tall glass of sweet tea, then sits at the kitchen table with Jada while I take out the ingredients and begin mixing them in a big bowl. "You girls are so sweet. Poor Honey lost her dad. She deserves something fancy and homemade."

My mouth pulls to the side. "Yes to the homemade part, but I'm not sure these qualify as fancy."

When the front door opens, Cricket barks to let me know that there's a new person in the house.

Honey trots to the front door to investigate.

My body stiffens, but when Phyllis strolls in, I relax, smiling at my little guard dogs.

I'm not sure I will ever get used to the fact that people in Apple Blossom Bay walk into each other's homes without warning or permission, and no one thinks that's odd.

"What a horrible day," Phyllis says by way of a greeting. Her robin's egg-colored ballgown swishes over her ankles as she saunters into the kitchen. "Did you hear about Hank?" She waves us off with her lace-colored arm before we can answer. "Of course you did. Larry told me you found his body, Hannah." She makes her way to me and kisses my cheek. "Bless you, little muffin. How awful! And you're baking? No, no. Sit down. Em, get her some sweet tea or something."

Phyllis opens the fridge and pulls out the sweet tea, then pours a glass. Instead of offering it to me, as she suggested, she takes a long drink. Then she fans herself as worry pinches between her brows.

She cringes. "I meant to pour this for you! I'm all turned around today. I blame whoever killed Hank."

I take in her distress with compassion. "I'm not thirsty, so no worries."

I love that this seventy-year-old woman wears ball gowns for no reason. I wish I had that confidence.

"Did you know Hank well?" I ask Phyllis, using my foot to pull out a chair at the table for her.

Phyllis smacks her lips and sets down her drink. "Did I know him well? You could say that. I knitted Honey's favorite blanket. I come over and help Hank when he gets all turned around in the kitchen. He helps me when my dish disposal acts up." She shakes her head. "Everyone looks after everyone here, but Hank was my friend. He had a lot of years left in him. He didn't deserve to leave this life so prematurely. Just awful."

Jada picks up the mixing bowl for me and gives the batter a stir while I add another tablespoon of dried ginger. "Any idea who might have wanted to hurt him? We're coming up empty over here."

Phyllis takes another long sip of the sweet tea. "Do you have a straw, honey?"

At mention of her name, Honey comes trotting back into the kitchen, though she doesn't go to Phyllis, but stays near me.

I grab a straw from the drawer and sink it into Phyllis' drink. "Hank's neighbor didn't seem too thrilled to see Honey. But I can't imagine someone wanting to kill a man because his dog peed on your petunias."

Phyllis chortles. "Those aren't just petunias," she tells me. "Those are prize-winning petunias. Bertie Filch won first place for those two years ago. Last year, she lost to her sister, Gertie." She shakes her head. "I'm not sure she ever forgave Hank for the withered state of those flowers last year. She's a sore loser." She waves at Honey. "I'm guessing Honey is staying here? That'll make Bertie happy."

I nod. "Just until Hank's family can decide what they want to do with Honey."

"You'd better hope they don't fight over that dog the way they're going to fight over that boat of his." Phyllis shivers as if the mention of Hank's family brings up bad memories. "He's got two children, and they fight to the death over nothing as it is. Give them an actual toy to bicker over? Forget it. They're never going to let this go."

Jada dumps the dough out onto the counter at my behest. "Fortunately, we don't have to deal with that. We get to spoil two dogs and call it a day. Em, where's your rolling pin?"

Jada grins with a thrill of glee. "Look at me! I'm going to use a rolling pin! I'm such a chef."

We snicker at Jada's claim, remembering that just a couple weeks ago, Em had to teach her how to make mashed potatoes. Again.

Aunt Em points to a cupboard on the left.

I take out the rolling pin and start flattening the brown dough, hoping that this will make useable, tasty dog biscuits. Then I hand the tool to Jada after demonstrating its use so she can give it a try. I want her to gain confidence in the kitchen.

I pick up the bowl and move it into the sink to give Jada more space. "So, it could be one of Hank's children behind the murder, if they wanted to get their hands on his boat."

Jada nods, processing my conjecture. "Sure. Or it could be Bertie Filch behind Hank's murder, if she was sore about losing last year because Honey peed on her flowers. Though, why she would wait this long to get her revenge makes no sense."

Phyllis motions outside the kitchen window to the tree beginning its bloom. "Actually, if it was Bertie for that reason, now would be the perfect time. The flower show is coming up. If she wanted to protect her petunias for the contest, now is the time for drastic action."

Jada frowns as she fishes a cup down from the cupboard. "But why murder Hank and not Honey? It's not like Hank is the one who was peeing on her flowers."

"True," I allow. "But if you're willing to murder over a flower contest, you're not exactly thinking rationally."

Jada and I cut and bake the dog biscuits into circles using the top of a cup as our cutter while Phyllis and Aunt Em discuss the last year's winner of the flower show, and then guess at who might win the prize this year.

By the time the biscuits are baked and cooled, and the dogs are munching happily on their ginger-flavored treats, Jada and I are no closer to solving Hank's murder than we were before we preheated the oven.

When Jada leaves for the evening, I can't shake the feeling that I am missing a crucial clue. While I might not have known Hank, I feel responsible for finding his killer. It's the least I can do after discovering his body.

As I wind down for bed, I pick up Cricket to sleep on the queen-sized mattress beside me, where she always rests at night. Then I do the same for Honey, who doesn't resist the assistance, nor her new sleeping arrangement.

I climb into the bed, cocooned between two dogs who happened into my life at just the right time. Cricket's fluffy tail flicks over my arm, while Honey licks my wrist to let me know she wants me close.

If there is a better feeling in the world than being

cuddled by two dogs, I do not know it. My heart attaches that much more firmly to Honey and Cricket.

Now I am certain that whatever it is they want, I will see to.

I need to figure out who killed Hank, so Honey has some closure. She deserves to know that whoever killed her best friend is now behind bars. As my dogs drift off to sleep, my mind races, wondering who could have hurt Hank, and left Honey without her dad.

7

NEW BOSS

For my first day on the job, I would say it's going far better than the interview. I haven't found a single dead body, and I have two dogs by my side the entire time.

I was worried this morning while I got dressed in my jeans and gray t-shirt that Larry might not remember he gave me permission to bring the dogs with me to work, but when he sees them, he greets Cricket as if they are old friends. That seems to be the nature of my sweet Pomeranian.

Honey, on the other hand, gets a wave from Larry but not a pat on the head. That seems to be the way Honey prefers things. She never growls or nips, but she shies away from people and clings tight to my ankles.

Larry doesn't even care if they're on a leash. "They

won't run off. They're both good dogs. Besides, the leashes will only slow you down while you work."

I like it here already.

It doesn't take long for Larry to give me a tour of the store, and then show me around the backroom, motioning for a list I need to follow to make sure things remain stocked in a timely fashion.

I love a good list and set to work on it without hesitation.

Larry is easy to work for, since he is grateful for any help he can get. His eyes are perpetually wide, even as he hands me the red vest that matches his, informing me that this is the uniform here. If Larry has noticed the fact that I have only my left hand, he hasn't mentioned anything about it.

It's such a relief not to be treated as if I cannot do the job I was hired to perform.

When I stock the pet food area, I frown at the high price of Honey's brand of food. It seems that Hank liked to give Honey the most expensive stuff in the store. Even at the local grocer's, the price is sky high.

I swallow hard, knowing that if I am going to take good care of Hank's dog, I can't go changing her dog food all willy-nilly. I need to bite the bullet and buy the good stuff, so Honey has an easier transition into her new home.

I didn't think I would love working at the grocery store this much, but my goodness, this is the place for me. All day long, I get to make sure the items on the shelves are perfectly in line, in between hugging both dogs, who stick by my side all morning.

The mood all around is somber whenever Larry comes by to check on me, so I dial down my pep marginally. After giving me the introductory spiel about how to clock in, the basic job description and what the objectives for the day are, he disappeared to the back to do his normal work. But when he strolls into my aisle to check on my progress a few hours later, his smile is halfhearted. "How's my favorite new employee?" he asks me, reaching down to pet Cricket.

I straighten the row of cereal boxes I am stocking while I answer. "So far, so good. I'm nearly done with this aisle."

Larry kneels to give Cricket a two-handed scratch behind her ears. "Not too boring over here? You're Em's niece, so I don't figure this is up to your usual excitement."

I smirk at the mention of my aunt. "She is always doing something fun."

"This town could use a little fun right now." Larry tilts his head at me. "How are you holding up? It can't be easy, after seeing Hank that way." He runs his hand over his face. "And right after he lost big at poker, too."

I lean into the information, since being mute when my new boss is opening up doesn't seem the way to go if I want to make friends here. "Hank lost money?"

Larry nods. "Now I feel terrible for being such a sore winner. I think I even did an 'I win' dance. Not the best way to remember the last day seeing your friend alive."

"You couldn't have known." I stack the last box of

cereal and stand back to admire my work. It's so satisfying to see things in a perfect row. "How much did you win?"

"Five hundred dollars."

I whistle, impressed that such high-stakes games go on in this small town. "I didn't realize you all played for more than quarters."

Larry's hand remains on Cricket, as if he needs the dog to keep him from clamming up. "Usually that's all we do. But every now and then, the game gets away from us. Paul kept pushing the pot higher. Put down his watch, then dared me to put in the deed to my Vespa." He rubs the nape of his neck. "Glad I didn't lose that one." Larry stands. His hands in his pockets make him look like a lost boy. "Paul kept pushing Hank to put in the deed for his boat, but Hank would rather fold than give that up."

I lean on the shelf. "Paul wanted Hank's boat?"

Larry shrugs. "Honestly, I think Paul just wanted to play big and have a little fun. It's all a game anyway. Hank lost some money that night, but not his boat." He sighs. "Now his kids are probably going to fight over it, which is a shame. It was Hank's peaceful place. His escape from the world. To think of his kids fighting over his peaceful place sort of undoes the whole point of the boat."

I gnaw on my lower lip. "Tell me more about Paul. Anyone who wants Hank to gamble away his serene escape might have more skin in the game than you realize."

Larry's expression pulls. "Paul? Nah. He's a joker. He

just wanted to have fun and got a little carried away with it. He spends all day at the bank, and cuts loose when it's just us."

I make a mental note to go to the bank after work.

Larry is pleasant to be around since he opens up so easily. It's like he's been waiting for an employee he can pal around with, even though he is the owner. He helps me unload a couple more boxes and even stocks the shelf beside me for a few, asking about city life and what it's like living with the famously spirited Emily Burton.

After Larry leaves to go do actual managerial work, I continue my chores with a little lift in my step.

Cricket and Honey don't go farther from my side than a few feet throughout the duration of my shift. Shoppers filter in and out, and as I help them find items in the store, I learn where they are myself for the first time.

I like the quiet work of stocking shelves. I almost wonder if I'd taken the path of getting a job like this straight out of high school, if I would have been happier these past several years. Or perhaps the reason I'm smiling while I work is because this town has a way of putting you where you feel like the best version of yourself.

After I clock out, I take my time strolling down the streets of the town, noting the quaint shops on the way to my destination. They all have quirky names and even more eclectic things to sell. I love the pots of flowers that dot the streets outside the various businesses. Many planters are lined with seashells to give shoppers the beachy feel.

I hadn't planned on going to the bank after work, but when Larry mentioned Paul is employed there, I know my very next move will be to open a bank account at the Apple Blossom Savings and Loan.

8

PAUL'S GOLD WATCH

$\mathcal{E}$ven the bank in Apple Blossom Bay is cuter than a normal financial establishment. There are several bird houses on the way to the entrance, and one is an exact replica of the bank itself.

I have both leashes attached to my belt with a small carabiner, ensuring I have my arms free and also that my dogs stay close.

There is a coffee cart run by a little old lady who smiles at me when I stroll in. "Is it okay if I bring my dogs inside?" I ask tentatively, pausing inside the door. Even though there is a sign on the glass that reads "Dogs Welcome", I have to doublecheck.

The woman is all smiles as she greets me. She couldn't weigh more than a hundred pounds. She's a tiny little thing. Her knobby fingers reach into the pink apron around her waist and pull out two dog bones. "Of course!

Cricket is one of our favorite customers. Come here, girl." She smiles at Honey but doesn't call her. "This is for Honey, but I know she won't take it unless Hank gives it to her." Her smile dims. "I heard about Hank's death. Are you adopting his dog?"

I shake my head. "I wish. I'm just watching her until Hank's family decides what they want to do."

The woman hands me the extra dog biscuit. "Here. See if she'll take it from you."

I lean down and kiss the top of Honey's head, then offer her the treat with a coo of encouragement.

Sure enough, Honey munches on the biscuit, but only so long as I kneel beside her. I love that it's not just me who needs her, but she relies on me, as well.

The woman clasps her hands under her chin. "Well, isn't that just the strangest thing. You're Hannah, right? Em's niece? The new girl from the big city who's staying with Emily."

I grin at the woman. "That's me. I figure I should think about opening a bank account. Larry told me that Paul is the best. Might he be available to talk with?"

"Oh, sure." She pours me a cup of coffee and offers the cream and sugar, but I politely decline the frills. "I'm Vera. You sit on down here while I get Paul for you."

I take one of the seats, not realizing until I sit down just how tired my legs are from standing and stocking shelves all day long.

When Paul comes out, I fight back a groan as I stand.

Paul is round and sweaty with a welcoming smile. "Good to meet you. Em is one of my favorite people, though I'm sure you hear that all the time. She made the birdhouses out front, you know."

My eyes widen. "They're adorable! I didn't realize my aunt made birdhouses."

"Oh, yes. There's really nothing Emily can't do." Paul shakes my wrist with a hearty grip. I always appreciate when people don't shy away from my missing hand. "You're Hannah, right? Em was talking up your arrival for weeks before you came into town."

"That's sweet of her. Yes, I'm Hannah Hart. Larry told me I should talk to you about possibly opening a bank account here, since I just started working at the Forgotten Stock Market."

"Larry's a good guy." Paul escorts me to his desk, which has a partition behind it so there is the illusion of privacy. "That sounds like something I can help you with. How much are we putting in there to start?"

I lean back in my seat, going for a direct connection so I can poke around at the real reason I came here—to see if Paul had anything to do with Hank's murder. "I'm not depositing as much as Larry won at poker on Friday night, that's for sure. Just somewhere my checks can be deposited."

Paul chuckles, but then he bows his head. "Larry cleaned up real good, but we lost Hank soon after. Had I known that was the last day we would see him, I wouldn't have given Hank such a hard time."

"A hard time? About what?"

Paul lowers his voice. "I wanted a bit of excitement, so I kept raising the bets beyond what we usually tolerate. I threw in this watch," he says, showing me his wrist. "It's solid gold, you know. I got it because I was supposed to retire, but retirement didn't take, so I came back here. We were having fun. Trying to feel alive, despite the evidence that we are a bunch of aging old farts."

I give him a polite smile while I wait for his story to hit the parts I know are coming.

I observe his movements as he fidgets with his collar. He doesn't look particularly guilty or capable of murder, but he doesn't exactly wreak of innocence, either.

Paul leans in, keeping his voice low. "Hank loves his fishing boat. It's a nice one, but it's better than most because he takes such meticulous care of it. I wanted him to throw in the deed to it, but he wouldn't. Maybe I pushed him a little too hard." Paul takes out a folder and opens it for me, displaying the literature of the bank but not explaining a lick of it. "Hank left when Larry won big. Didn't look too thrilled that I pushed the poker game so far over the edge."

I point to his watch. "How do you have your watch if Larry won?"

Paul chuckles. "I bought it back from him the very morning Hank's body was found, actually. I asked Larry to come into the bank before he opened his store, and we traded money for my watch. Larry's a good guy."

I nod. "So, the morning Hank was found murdered, Larry was with you?"

That crosses Larry off the list. Though, after spending some time with him, he wasn't in my mind as a potential murderer. He's too amiable to be bad to the core.

Paul studies me, as if seeing my appearance here in a new light. "You're the girl who found Hank, aren't you."

My head bobs. "I can't imagine who would hurt Hank like that. Though, I'm guessing you knew Hank better than most. Any ideas who might have had it out for him?"

Paul shakes his head. "No one who knew him well would ever hurt him. Hank's a good person. Liked to fish and dote on Honey, there." He waves at Honey, who whines and tucks her head behind my leg. "Hank's kids are coming into town to deal with his things and whatnot. I would guess a great deal of fighting is going to break out over his boat. But both his kids live out of state, so I can't imagine either of them could have been capable of harming Hank, being that they weren't nearby. But boy, if they lived closer, I wouldn't have put it past either of them to do something a better person would regret."

I swallow hard. "I want to find out who did this, so it doesn't happen again."

Paul shuffles a few papers on his desk. "Let me know how I can help." He leans in. "You might want to talk to Dave. He's our fourth for poker nights. He walked Hank out when he folded and decided to leave for the evening. Maybe Dave saw or heard something of note."

I tuck that nugget of information away as Paul shifts tunes.

"So, let's see to getting you a bank account." He smiles welcomingly at me. "Then you're *really* a resident here."

I nod along and fill out the necessary paperwork, all the while wondering how this poker night got so far out of control that vespas, gold watches, boats, and possibly lives were on the line.

9

SISTERS OF SCANDAL

When I get home, I hear a smattering of shushing as I cross over the threshold with my dogs by my side. "Aunt Em?" I call out, wondering what she could possibly be up to that requires secrecy.

"It's fine! I'm telling you, it's fine." I hear my aunt say to whomever she is with in the kitchen.

My brow quirks as I move with tentative steps toward the voices. "Is everything okay?"

Cricket has no qualms about there being something going on in the house. She pants happily, snorting a few times as she trots into the kitchen ahead of me. When there are no signs of growling or upset, I follow behind with Honey at my heels.

"Oh, hello Phyllis." I glance around the kitchen, my gaze landing on a piece of paper spread out on the tabletop.

"Hi, sweetie. Come on in." Phyllis waves me into the kitchen with a flick of her lace glove-covered hand. Then she says to my aunt, "Remind me to pick up peaches. I need to make more jam."

I take in the face of Edna, who waves me forward, and a fourth—a woman I have not yet met. "Hi. I'm Hannah Hart, Emily's niece."

The woman looks to be in her seventies, alongside Phyllis, only she doesn't have the roundness to her face nor the penchant for lavish gowns that Phyllis possesses. "I'm Dorothy," she informs me with a small smile lifting the corners of her wide mouth. "I've known your aunt since she was a wee one. I was out of town last month, or I would have stopped by sooner to give you a proper welcome." Dorothy can't possibly weigh more than a hundred pounds with her dainty, wiry features. She stands barely over five feet tall when she rises to greet me with a hug.

I'm still getting used to this small town, wherein people hug each other for no reason. "It's nice to meet you." I decide to try my hand at polite chitchat. "Out of town? That sounds nice. Where were you visiting?"

Dorothy beams at me, announcing her traveling with pride. "I have a life goal of visiting every interesting bookstore in the country. I took a bus to see a bookstore that's inside an old bank. It was gorgeous!" Her eyes widen with intrigue. "Fourteen murders took place there. Can you imagine?"

My mouth pops open as I fight to keep up. "When it was a bank or when it was a bookstore?"

Dorothy pats my forearm. "Mostly when it was a bank, but one when it was a bookstore. Interesting, right? At this one, they had sculptures inside made of damaged books. So beautiful!"

Em casts me a "You'll get the hang of my friends soon enough" sort of look. "Dorothy has visited dozens of oddball bookstores all over the country. She brings Phyllis, Edna, and me back a book from each one to add to our collection." She reaches up and pulls down a hardcover from atop the fridge. "See? She's searching for the whole collection of *The Wizard of Oz* books for me, buying one at a time from her various travels."

My shoulders lower as the sweet life goal washes over me. "I love that." My mouth pulls to the side. "I can't think of a single thing I am that passionate about, where I would travel the country to see various bookstores."

Dorothy gives me another squeeze. "Don't worry, Hannah Hart. You'll find your crazy bookstore."

Dorothy keeps her arm wound around my back as she angles her body toward the table. "You're just in time. If you're Em's niece, then you're one of us." She motions to the table, which looks to have a paper with a list growing on the lines. "Best jump into the deep end with both feet. We're planning a heist!"

She declares it so proudly; I'm not sure how to react. "Um, what?"

Phyllis stands, revealing her ballgown that is bright yellow with lace details from frilled collar to ankle-length hem. She looks to Em, to Edna, and then to Dorothy, who each nod eagerly. "It's time we usher in a new generation of sisters."

Edna motions to my aunt's cell phone on the counter. "Em, call Jada and have her come over. Phyllis is right; we need to pass on our wisdom to these girls. We can't keep all the fun for ourselves."

My mouth falls open while Cricket yips excitedly, declaring that she wants in on whatever Phyllis is offering.

Honey is not so sure.

Neither am I.

"A heist?" I echo in a warbly voice, my knees weakening under the weight of this impending crime.

Phyllis nods, spreading out her arms. "Welcome to the Sisters of Scandal."

I chew on my lower lip, unsure what to do with Phyllis' invitation. I didn't even know the Sisters of Scandal existed. I am the last person on the planet who should be extended an invite to something with the word "scandal" in it. "I don't know, Phyllis. This is your club, and I'm not exactly adventurous."

Aunt Em moves to my other side while Dorothy squeezes my shoulder excitedly. "We can fix that. You want to do something good for yourself?" Em jerks her chin toward her two friends. "This is it."

My aunt's perpetual reminder to do something good

for myself beckons me forward, but my feet stop after one timid step toward the table. "Why me?" I ask, my voice choked and quiet, certain they are betting on the wrong horse.

Aunt Em straightens her spine as if I have insulted her by not believing in my own value. "Because you are worth taking a gamble on, Hannah Grapefruit. You need a smile that's yours. A smile you put on your own face, not one that's prescribed to you."

Phyllis and Edna nod in unison as Dorothy grasps my forearm. "It's time we bring in a new generation. It's not going to do this town any good if the four of us are the only ones shaking things up around here. We need to pass down our wisdom. It would be selfish not to."

Phyllis doesn't seem to hold an ounce of caution anywhere in her wrinkled body. She nods with gusto, a smile teasing the creased corners of her mouth. "I agree. Hannah, you need this. You need us. If we don't take you in and teach you the way to go, you're going to go through your whole life as a rule follower."

The four of them shudder.

I tilt my head at Phyllis. "There's nothing wrong with being good."

Phyllis shakes her finger at me. "Being a rule follower is not the same thing as being good. You can break lots of rules if they're the ones that keep you from doing the most amount of good."

"I don't understand." Or perhaps I don't want to understand.

Aunt Em nods soberly. "It's worse than I thought." Her arms grip my shoulders. "It's time you learned how to do things the way of the Sisters of Scandal."

I chew on my lower lip, unsure what sort of sorority I am being brought into, and just what fell deeds will be expected of me.

Aunt Em nods to Phyllis. "I'm taking Hannah under my wing."

Phyllis straightens. "I'll call Jada and take her under mine. She's been ready to join for a while. The girls can help each other find their way."

Dorothy's mouth pulls to the side as she elbows Edna. "That leaves you and me on the lookout for a young woman in need of corruption."

"Direction, you mean," I correct Dorothy.

She tilts her head at me. "That's what I said."

It's a short phone call and ten minutes later that Jada shows up on our doorstep wearing a black cloak, I'm guessing for dramatic effect. "I'm ready to join the Sisterhood of Scandal," she announces in an ominous voice after she lets herself inside.

Her presence sets off Cricket's impertinent barking until Jada pets her.

Honey isn't sure about any of this, and neither am I.

Dorothy holds her hands over the table while Phyllis smooths out the paper. "Girls, some towns get by just fine living life by the book. But Apple Blossom Bay needs a little push every now and then. That's what the Sisterhood of Scandal is here for."

Jada holds my hand, gleeful that this day of induction has finally come. I can tell she has been waiting for this moment for quite some time and doesn't hold the same reservations I do.

Phyllis' eyes water as she gazes at the two of us. "I was a much younger girl when Em, Edna, Dorothy and I started up our mischief. I would have gone down a far more trodden path, had these three not saved me from myself."

"I'm not doing anything illegal," I blurt out, letting all the air out of the room.

Aunt Em's hazel eyes twinkle playfully. "I think you might, once you hear what we're planning."

I hold my breath, unsure what to make of these women and the secret society they have cooked up behind the scenes of this cozy small town.

10

MY FIRST FELONY

"I'm not sure about this!" I fret as I tiptoe into City Hall in the dead of night.

Actually, I am *very* sure about this. Sure that this is a bad idea, and that we shouldn't be attempting something illegal by moonlight.

When Phyllis, Edna, Dorothy and Aunt Em told Jada and me that our job as junior members of the Sisterhood of Scandal would be to break into City Hall at midnight and sneak out the sound system, I should have put my foot down. But there's something about being asked so sweetly by four older women that makes my protests sound like the feeble ramblings of a girl who has never truly lived.

Which is not far off the mark, come to think of it.

My caveat that I would not wiggle on is that I am taking my dogs with me. I'm sure they assumed I wanted canine backup during my bout of thievery with Jada, but really, it's because I don't like being out of the house without my dogs. They give me the confidence to be my most normal self.

Which, apparently, is a thief tonight.

Jada's giggling isn't helping my nerves. "I'm so excited! It's my first petty crime."

Sweat dampens the nape of my neck. "This was a bad idea. We're not stealing bubble gum; this is a sound system!" I examine the bulky obsidian equipment under the beam of my flashlight, my stomach in knots. "This is part of it, but is this?" I motion to a pile of cords.

Jada shrugs. "Let's take it all."

"You do realize that everything we steal is added up if we get caught, right? The fewer items we take, the better. It could be the difference between community service and jail time."

Jada bats away my worry as she unplugs several wires from the wall underneath the desk at the back of the main room. It looks like conferences and town meetings are held here at City Hall, for which they would very much need their sound system, and notice if it went missing.

Jada keeps her eyes on the wires, flicking back the edge of her cloak. "But if we don't get all we need, we'll have to break in all over again, which increases our chances of getting caught."

I whisper shout at her. "This was a bad idea!"

She holds her flashlight between her teeth as she hefts up a control board, and then jerks her head toward a giant speaker near the wall.

My mouth drops open. "That's not going to fit in my car!"

Jada brings the sound board to the exit and sets it down, moving the flashlight from her mouth to her fist. "That's why I have my car, too. Between the two of us, we can get it all."

Cricket wags her tail as if this is all great fun. She and Honey move together, sniffing out the corners of the room.

I fan my face as sweat runs down my temple. "Do you hear yourself? Stealing is not a victimless crime!"

"Sure it is, if we plan to give it all back." Jada sizes up my freakout and grabs my shoulders, looking me square in the eye in the dark. Her face is lit only by the red glow of the exit sign by the door and our flashlights. "Listen, Hannah Hart. You're freaking out. If we don't do this, Hank won't get the proper sendoff he deserves. This matters, not just for him, but for the whole town."

"I might be sick," I warn her.

"We need to live." She purses her lips together, reminding me of the real reason we're doing this. "I don't know about you, but I don't want to wake up in thirty years and wonder when the last time was that I truly felt alive. I want to live now." She pauses and narrows an eye at my squeamish nature. "And you're going to help me get there."

There is a wild quality to Jada's rounded umber eyes. Her desperation isn't just the insistence of a girl wanting to shake things up. This is Jada on the verge of an existential crisis.

If I was bolder, braver, I would voice the fact that I've been on the ledge, too, feeling the void of wishing I could do more, be more.

Be anything, really.

Though we are still new to each other, my heart goes out to Jada, meeting her where she's at so she does not have to feel the desperation of finding oneself on her own.

No, we will do this together.

I nod several times before my mouth opens, summoning what little courage I keep in my back pocket. "Okay. Yes. We can do this. We're giving all this stuff back once we're finished with it. There aren't any meetings scheduled here for the next week, so we'll get it all back in plenty of time."

Or we'll be arrested and rot in jail together.

Jada hugs me tight, marrying my heart to hers. "We need this," she insists. "Thank you for being wild with me."

"Thank you for committing a felony with me."

Cricket barks twice, letting us know she is happy to be along for the ride.

Honey whimpers in my direction, reminding us that heists should be done quickly without the lingering and chatting we are doing now.

Jada giggles as she releases me. "If this goes south, Em has bail money." She taps her temple knowingly, as if the presence of bail money should give me cheer.

We trot to the large speaker and lift it together, bringing it out the side door.

I expect Deputy Hanson to shine a floodlight on us, and for a police car to be our ride out of here. Perhaps there will be a helicopter with a megaphone announcing our sins to the entire town.

But the night is quiet, save for Cricket's snorty breaths that fill the midnight air and the jingle of Honey's collar. Jada and I struggle to move the massive speaker, but we manage to load it in without incident.

The hair on the back of my neck stands on end as the cool air prickles my skin. "You'll be in the jail cell with me if we get caught?" I ask her, needing to hear that my life spent mostly alone isn't going to be forever that way. Maybe I'll get caught and held to account, but perhaps this is the stuff from which lifelong bonds of friendship are made.

Perhaps this is what my soul has been waiting for, lying dormant until my aunt pushed Jada and me over the edge of our carefully planned lives.

Jada nods with equal parts relief and determination. "Sisters of Scandal all the way."

We load up the sound system with all its parts (I hope, because I am not coming back here), and drive carefully away from the scene of the crime.

I just committed my first felony.

And I also found a friend willing to be with me, even when the road gets rocky and my courage threatens to desert us completely.

If Jada can be wild, then maybe I can, too.

11

WHY I MAKE DOG TREATS

After work the next day, I bring home a grocery bag filled with all the ingredients to make another batch of dog biscuits. While I unload, letting Honey and Cricket sniff each item to verify the contents, Aunt Em, Dorothy, Edna, and Phyllis enter in through the backdoor of the house, laughing with each other.

I love the look of happiness on my aunt. After soaking in the May sunshine as they have been doing, I can't imagine anyone finding a reason to be depressed.

Aunt Em kisses my cheek. "Welcome home, Hannah Grapefruit. How was work?"

"Is it wrong that I love putting things in order? Like, really love it? Like, I can't wait to clock in tomorrow so I can see what needs to be straightened and stocked?" I grimace at how dorky that sounds.

Phyllis chortles at me as she sits at the table. "Oh,

goodness. I'm glad Larry has you. He was spinning his wheels for a while when he had to let Wally go."

"What was Wally fired for?" I ask, prying into something that really isn't any of my business. I take my time putting the groceries away.

Phyllis shakes her head. "Larry found him stealing from the register. Not good."

I cringe at my own theft that took place just last night. "Yikes. I'm sorry to hear that."

Dorothy snoops in my grocery bag. "What are you making, Hannah?"

"Phyllis, you were saying you wanted to make peach jam, so I thought you could use some peaches. The rest is ingredients to make more biscuits for the dogs."

Phyllis chuckles at me. "You didn't have to do that, Hannah. But thank you. I'll drop off a jar of jam after it's finished."

"I was hoping I could bribe you." I smirk at her. Phyllis makes the best jam in the world, and we're down to a quarter of a jar left. That won't do.

I place the peaches in a reusable grocery bag and set it near Phyllis' purse so she doesn't forget to take them home. "Do I want to know how many people are upset that Jada and I stole the sound system?"

Aunt Em bats away my worry. "Not a soul. I told you, no one is using City Hall this week. It's the perfect time for some low-stakes theft. Only steal what people won't miss."

I shoot my aunt a withering look. "I think they'll miss a sound system."

Edna pinches my cheek, as if my concern is cute. "Not if we put it back before the next meeting."

The four sit at the table and chat animatedly with each other while I get out the mixing bowl and start in on my evening baking project.

Dorothy and Phyllis knit, Edna crochets, and Aunt Em takes one of her broken planter pots from outside and sets to gluing it back together on the kitchen table. I love that they chat while they craft. It's a truly beautiful mix of productivity and relaxation.

While I measure out the flour, Em and Dorothy get out a set of paints, together deciding that the purple planter needs a new look.

I love the calming click of Phyllis' knitting needles, the pull of the yarn while Edna crochets, the melodic humming that escapes my aunt's pursed lips while she paints, and the scratching of a marker while Dorothy sketches a new design on the ceramic, having abandoned her knitting to assist my aunt.

It's not long before the kitchen smells of peanut butter and ginger, which is a truly huggable scent. When I add half a jar of peanut butter all in one go, I can't help but smile. There are few times in life where that amount of peanut butter can be used without it being excessive.

If only every day could have necessary excessive deliciousness.

Honey whines while she drools on my foot, which doesn't bother me in the least. I love that she sticks so close to me.

"You're happy," Phyllis comments while she knits, motioning with her chin to my gently swaying hips. "You're dancing while you bake."

I take in a deep, contented breath. "I can't help it. I'm not a terribly talented chef, but I love baking biscuits for my babies."

"Are they out of dog treats at the store?" Dorothy asks me while she draws an orchid on the side of the planter for Aunt Em to paint.

Cricket sneezes at Dorothy's suggestion, clearly preferring my homemade biscuits.

"No, but this is what I need to do."

"Need?" Dorothy inquires, not unkindly.

I nod, kneading the ingredients with my hand and arm, not flinching at the stickiness that I hope will come nicely together. "It's important to me that they get something that I made myself. I love these dogs. Not appreciate, not tolerate. I *love* them." I keep my eyes on the metal mixing bowl. "Why do you like making jam, Phyllis? Why do you love visiting odd bookstores, Dorothy? And what about you, Em? You love your plants. What about you, Edna?"

Edna grins at me. "I'm an ocean girl. I surf better than the teenagers, and swim nearly every morning before the sun rises. I love it. Makes me feel alive."

I motion to the others. "What about you ladies? Why do you love the things you do?"

Phyllis sets down her knitting needles, giving my question some thought. "Because jam just is. There's no purpose for jam, other than pure enjoyment. It doesn't fulfill any daily nutritional requirements, but if you're missing it, your kitchen is severely lacking joy. I love how unnecessary it is. I think, oddly enough, that's what makes it necessary to me. I need a little nonsense. A little joy. A little sugar."

Dorothy's voice is quiet and contemplative as she answers my question. "I'm dyslexic."

I turn, my hand frozen in the dough as I gape at her.

"I wasn't diagnosed until I was an adult, but that's the size of it. My parents wrote me off as stupid, but I knew I wasn't." She holds up her hand at my gasp. "They didn't know any better. But they wouldn't take me to the library, and wouldn't waste money on anything other than school books until I got my reading marks up, which I never did. Oh, I can read bits and pieces now. I do a lot of audio-books, actually."

My eyes mist over. "You visit bookstores now because you couldn't when you were a little girl?"

"I suppose so. Really, I want to hold a book. I want to see stacks of them in neat little rows. I want to see them shelved in odd buildings. I want to go into the place where I wasn't welcome when I was a little girl. Now that I can do anything I want, I know I want to be a person who appreciates books, even if I can't read them all without help."

I set down the mixing bowl and clear the gap between myself and Dorothy, giving her as much of a hug with my sticky limbs as possible without getting anything on her pink shirt. "I think that's amazing."

Dorothy chortles, patting my back. "I think you're right. I am amazing." When I pull back, she passes the conversation to Aunt Em. "Your turn, Plant Queen."

Aunt Em sets her paints down, staring at the leaves on her four-inch-tall plant as if she is addressing it instead of us. "My sister is good at everything."

It's a blanket statement that I don't argue. My mother is good at everything, and she makes sure you know it.

"I wasn't. I was 'weird'. I was 'wild'. I was…" I know she is searching for a label to describe her transgender identity. "I was different. But plants don't care about that. They grow no matter who is watering them. Girl, boy, man, woman, or a label in between. A plant lives for the sun and for water, just like me."

My heart squeezes with emotion that I cannot put into words.

Instead of giving these women who dared be vulnerable a passing answer of "I love dogs" as an adequate explanation of why I am making dog biscuits rather than buying them, I go for brutal honesty.

"I have wanted a dog of my very own my entire life. I've been planning and researching and practicing for the day that a dog happened into my life." My voice turns tender when I think back to my days in the big city. "There was a stray who came by the gas station where I worked every day. I practiced on him, wishing I could take him home with me. I baked him biscuits like these and took my lunch breaks with him. I told myself that if I ever was lucky enough to have a dog of my own, I would let them know how long I've wanted them. Homemade biscuits seem the way to communicate that." I shake my head. "I can't buy them biscuits because then the dogs might not taste how much I love them. They might not know how long I've dreamed of having this sort of companionship." I keep my eyes on my mixing bowl. "I was alone most of my childhood and on into adulthood. I was the 'weird' kid with the missing hand. Then I was the 'weird' bisexual teenager. I played checkers by myself, if you imagine. I don't know how to talk to people in the same way I can talk to dogs. I know Honey isn't mine to keep, but for this small space of time, I can pretend she is." My voice lowers to a whisper. "It's the best game of pretend I've ever played."

Often these days, I wonder if I should pinch myself because this is all such a marvelous dream. But if it is a dream, I don't want to wake from it. I want to put all the love I can into these babies who let me dote on them.

When I catch sight of the four women staring at my open heart, I clear my throat. "Um, so that's why I like making dog treats."

Cricket yips at the mention of her favorite word.

Aunt Em studies me with new appreciation. "I love that. See? I knew you were a Sister of Scandal. That's the stuff life is made of. Sure, the big moments are important, but it's the in between moments that make us. It's the pockets of joy we invent for no reason that make us human. You belong, Hannah." She kisses my cheek. "You belong with us."

Cricket barks in agreement.

Phyllis laughs. "See? Cricket knows what I'm talking about." She leans down and pets Cricket, then winks at Honey. "I was going to head to Puzzles and Pins with Edna this evening. Feel like joining us?"

I nod without holding back my interest. "You know that's my favorite thing to do. I need to exchange the puzzle I checked out and get a new one. Would the girls there mind if Honey tagged along with Cricket and me?"

Phyllis goes back to her knitting. "I think they'd prefer it."

Aunt Em keeps her eyes on her planter while she talks. "I passed by that strip of stores this morning. Saw Paul on his break. His eyes were red. Poor thing."

I roll out the dough until it's half an inch thick and then start cutting out star shapes using the play-dough cutter Jada let me borrow. "It's got to be hard to lose a friend so suddenly."

Aunt Em nods. "Not just that. Paul was upset, so I offered him a tissue. He said that he and Hank were supposed to go fishing together this weekend, but now they can't. It's all hitting him hard today."

Phyllis' knitting needles click in a soothing rhythm. "I think Paul regrets pushing that last game so far."

Em nods. "He told me exactly that. Paul regrets being so obnoxious during their last game of poker. They don't want to have another guys' night without Hank."

Dorothy sets down the writing utensil. "That makes sense."

Phyllis' mouth firms. "That's just silly. They need that game. It's the only thing Larry does that's just for fun. If the fun goes out of Apple Blossom Bay, then what do we have left?" She shakes her head. "A fat lot of nothing. I'll talk to Larry. Make him see what's what. They'll need a fourth to take Hank's seat."

Edna motions to me. "They should do what we're doing. They need to take in a younger member, so they don't get old sooner than they should. Paul, Larry and Dave need to replace Hank's seat at the table with someone younger who could use the camaraderie and corruption."

I snort at Edna's phrasing. Gotta love their priorities.

Aunt Em nods while I shove the baking sheet into the oven and then set the timer.

I motion to the three of them. "I'm starting to under-stand more and more why this Sisterhood of Scandal is important," I tell the women as I start to clean up my mess.

Dorothy straightens. "That's good. It's not just about

mischief and mayhem. It's about bringing life to those of us who need a little cheer. When things like this happen—one of our own dying so horribly—the sisterhood is needed now more than ever."

I am grateful that I get a peek at one of the reasons this small town is so very special. I let my mind drift, thinking up how I can add to the plan the sisterhood has mapped out on Phyllis' sheet of paper, now that I'm not worried about being arrested.

I want to be part of what makes this town come alive, even if it means risking getting caught. Even if it means being vulnerable and letting these women truly know the awkward person I have always been.

12

BICKERING SIBLINGS

After my shift at the grocery store the next day, I decide it's a good time to visit Jada. I even bought a small box of cookies with my employee discount for us to split. I switched out my purse for my backpack, so I could carry the cookies and still have my arms free.

I love that my two dogs follow me wherever I go. I never had this much courage when I lived in the big city. Now that I have the ocean air and my dogs on either side of me, I can smile and make eye contact while I walk. I can wave at the few people I sort of recognize from them coming into the grocery store and petting the dogs while they shop.

In fact, today I am no longer wearing my old jeans and faded gray t-shirt. I look like I belong at the bay in my cut-offs and pink tank top that I borrowed from Aunt Em. My curls are twisted in a fluffy bun atop my head. The sun is shining on my skin, and the breeze awakens whatever weariness might have wanted to settle in after an eight-hour shift. The boats are in their neat little rows on either side of the dock, with one boat in particular off to the side, where I aim my steps.

Before I reach Jada's houseboat, arguing hits my ears, turning my head. It's odd to hear raised voices in Apple Blossom Bay. Everyone is usually so amiable.

My footsteps slow as Honey clings tighter to my ankles, whining with her tail between her legs because she enjoys conflict about as much as I do. Cricket, on the other hand, has no idea that anything upsetting is being shouted. She pants happily, her bushy backside wagging as if life is one big series of games.

Gotta love her.

"You don't want the boat, Bradley. My gosh, what a dumb argument. You get seasick! When was the last time you were on the water?" A blonde woman shouts.

The man on the dock beside her with a matching hue of hair shouts just as loudly, though their proximity requires no heightened volume. "I don't want to keep it any more than you do. I want to sell it! And forgive me, but going on a cruise for your vacation last year hardly makes you sea-sturdy. Give me a break."

There is a third person, a man in a suit, standing a few feet from the two with his most patient expression plastered in place. "If you both would listen to what the will states, you might…"

The woman's voice shoots up an octave. "The will doesn't matter if the two of us agree. I should have the boat!"

The man in the suit must be the lawyer, I'm guessing.

While I generally shy away from big dramatic displays like the one unfolding on the dock, I actually am grateful that the lawyer for Hank's estate is here.

I've got a question that's been burning in my soul ever since I laid eyes on Honey.

I meander toward him, flagging him down while the man and the woman go at each other with what can only be described as pure vitriol. "Hi, sir. I'm Hannah Hart. Sorry to bother you. Are you the lawyer for Hank's estate?"

The man produces a business card. He looks to be in his forties, but if the bags under his eyes were gone, I'm guessing he could be in his thirties. "I am. Javier Rodriquez. Is there something I can help you with?"

He looks grateful for any interruption because it will give him a break from the argument that seems to have no end in sight.

I adjust my backpack and draw myself up, even though my natural inclination is to run away. I might not be able to be bold for myself, but when it comes to these two dogs, I know I can find my voice.

"I'm glad I ran into you. I'm the one who found Hank's body. His dog, Honey, was with him, poor thing." I motion to the doe-eyed corgi who couldn't be more loveable if she tried. "I didn't want Honey to have to go to a shelter, so I took her home with me. Is that okay?" I hold up my hand. "I know I'll have to give her to one of his kids, but for now, until things are settled, is it okay if I keep her with me? Deputy Hanson said that would be alright, but maybe you're the one to talk to, as well."

Javier tilts his head at the dog and then at me. "Hannah, you said?"

I nod. "Hannah Hart. Honey's been staying with me since Hank passed."

But that's not all I want to say. I debate chickening out, but it's as if Honey can sense my nerves, because she whines to remind me that this isn't about me; it's about her.

Maybe I can't be brave for myself, but I can do it for her.

I lean in, whispering so Honey doesn't hear the difficult conversation. "If Hank's kids don't want Honey, how do I go about requesting to keep her?"

There. I said it. I asked for what I wanted. My pulse races and my mouth is dry, but I did it.

Though I know I only asked Aunt Em if Honey could stay with us temporarily, my heart would break if I had the opportunity to keep this sweet corgi but had to give her back simply because I didn't ask.

Javier jerks his chin toward the two arguing people by Hank's boat. "Let's ask them right now. If they don't want to take Honey home, as far as I'm concerned, she's all yours.

That was nice of you—taking Honey in so she didn't have to go to a kennel."

Even though I have them both on leashes that are attached to my belt loop with my trusty carabiner, my dogs follow me without being told, leaving plenty of slack. My plan is to wait to speak until the two siblings have a lull in their fight, but that doesn't seem to be happening.

"You have enough money, Bradley! I saw your car."

"You don't need the money from the sale of this boat, Hattie. I swear, you have no idea what to do with the money you have. You spend it quicker than you can earn it."

Finally, Javier intervenes. "Hattie, Bradley, this is Hannah Hart. She's been watching your father's dog since Hank passed. Normally, the dog would go to one of you. Do either of you wish to take Honey home with you?"

Hattie's nose scrunches. "Are you serious? Bradley wants the boat, and I would be stuck with the dog? No way. That dog is a money suck. All dogs, really." She holds up her hand when Bradley protests. "I have kids. I can't take the dog."

Bradley guffaws. "I live in an apartment where they don't allow dogs. Nice try, Hattie. You're taking the dog."

I hold up my hand like a child asking for permission to sit at the grown-up table.

When that doesn't stop their bickering, I switch arms, holding up my right which is missing a hand.

Sure enough, the sight draws their eyes and closes

their mouths so I can make my case for Honey. "Excuse me, but if neither of you want to take Honey, would it be okay if I kept her? I can take care of her, and she's already comfortable with me. I've been looking after her since..."

But that's all the explanation they need.

Bradley and Hattie surprise me by having what I am guessing is their first ever agreement. "Done," they say in unison. Then Hattie adds, "We're not paying for food or anything. You take the dog, she's your responsibility."

I nod so quick; I am certain my eyes rattle. "Absolutely. Thank you!"

Emotion sweeps over me, warming my insides and lifting my spirits so much that I feel as if I am soaring. I guide my dogs a few feet away from the three further down the dock, so I don't openly weep in front of strangers.

I kneel beside my dogs, welcoming them both to kiss my face while I wrap my arms around them. "You're coming home to stay, Honey! This is the best day ever! What do you think, Cricket? Should we go on an extra-long walk to celebrate?"

Cricket is filled with energy and needs no coaxing to jump and dance around with her tongue hanging out.

Absolute ham.

Honey leans into my embrace, marrying my heart to hers.

Javier smiles down at me, distancing himself from the siblings who have resumed their bickering. "My office's address is on the card I gave you. Tomorrow, could you stop by? I can give you a transfer of ownership form, so Honey will be officially yours."

My eyes glisten with gratitude as I stand. "Thank you! Tomorrow I might be busy. The day after?"

Busy, as in, putting together puzzles with Phyllis, Edna and Lorraine at Puzzles and Pins.

Javier nods. "That'll work."

"I'll be there." The urge to throw my arms around this stranger is strong, but I hold myself back. "Thank you so much. I'll be at your office after I get off work."

When Javier turns back to deal with the squabbling siblings, I skip toward Jada's houseboat, which was the reason I came down here to begin with. I cannot wait to tell her the amazing news.

I did it. I did something good for myself.

Sisterhood of Scandal, indeed.

"Jada!" I call out as I teeter on the edge of the dock, looking for the steps. When I don't see them, I judge the distance to be only a few feet down, but I wager I shouldn't jump.

Instead, I get down on my knees and turn my body, dangling my legs. My toes try to feel for the solid surface, but the platform for the houseboat is a few feet away from the dock, so I'm not close enough to lower myself with any real certainty.

"I can't swim," I confess to my dogs. "I'll get on the houseboat first, then I'll reach for you two." I abandon their leashes on the dock, unhooking them so I don't accidentally pull them overboard before I am ready for them.

My dogs bark at me, asking what on earth I am attempting, when a male voice calls to me from behind. "Breaking and entering is a crime, you know."

Terror grips me around the throat. "Ah!" My elbows unlock, turning to jelly while my lower half scrambles to make a solid surface out of pure water.

My hand slips from the edge of the dock, and I miss the boat by several feet. I cry out as my entire body drops into the water, immersing me in Apple Blossom Bay's cold ocean.

Where I rapidly start to sink.

13

DROWNING

I cannot swim, and I am about to be arrested.

I'm not sure if drowning or going to jail is worse, so nature gets to decide. If I live, whoever yelled out to tell me they caught me breaking and entering (clearly knowing that Jada and I stole the sound equipment), is going to arrest me.

My arms cut through the water over and over while my legs kick haphazardly. My body sinks even though I am aiming for the surface. I have no idea what I'm doing.

This is how I am going to die.

My backpack only has my wallet, a bottle of water and the box of cookies I bought to bring to Jada, but right now, it feels like a waterlogged weight, anchoring me toward the bottom of the ocean.

I spot the platform of the houseboat, as well as the posts of the dock. I see which way is up, but I am not sure I can figure out how to get there, even as I punch my arms through the water without a measure of rhythm to my movements.

A body plunges into the water beside me, though I don't see who it is. An arm goes around my waist as my lungs remind me that I am not a mermaid. I need air, and soon.

Though I am uncertain of most things in life at this point, I trust that the arm around me knows more about swimming than I do (which isn't saying much). I am jerked to the surface, my lungs thanking the person who saved me when they are finally able to gulp in some fresh air.

Inch-long wet black hair stands back from the forehead of a man a couple years older than me whom I recognize to be Jada's brother.

Jada's extraordinarily handsome brother.

I shriek my horror that someone this good looking is keeping me afloat. I want to get far away so I don't do anything stupid, but that would involve drowning. "Niles?" I splutter as I cough directly into his face. "What are you…"

His arms are strong, his biceps tight around me, fulfilling a fantasy I didn't realize I had. Not even my daydreams are this bold, but I'm sure they will be after today.

I wish I didn't know what his arms felt like, wrapped around me. It's the best thing in the world, which means I need to get far, far away before I do or say something stupid.

Niles grabs onto the platform of his sister's houseboat. "Hold onto me. I've got you." His brown eyes are wild with concern. "I didn't mean to make you fall. You still can't swim?"

It's then that I remember how I landed myself in such a precarious position. "You scared me! I thought you were a policeman, coming to arrest me for breaking and entering!" My chest heaves while my tired arm clings to the edge of the wooden platform.

Niles shoots me a wry look. "You know, if you don't actually do any breaking and entering, that's not something you have to worry about being arrested for."

I can't tell if he's being glib or if he knows that I broke into City Hall and stole their sound system with his sister.

Did Jada tell him? Does Niles know that I'm a felon? The weight of his possible disapproval sits heavy on my chest.

Cricket and Honey bark for me, startling me so much that I lose my hold on the platform. I scream as my head dips under the water, and consequently take in a mouthful of the ocean.

Niles grabs my wrist and tugs me back up before I can plummet too far. "Okay, first things first," he says when my head is above water once more. "We're getting you on solid ground, and then we're getting you swimming lessons."

My hand smacks on the edge of the houseboat's base. I am just turned around enough to let my sass show. "How about you don't scare me when I am trying to get to your sister's house? Then I won't fall into the water, and this won't be a tissue!"

Niles tilts his head to the side, as if this is the moment I should be called out for my verbal error. "A tissue?"

"An issue!" I shout, growling at my ineptitude. "You know what I mean."

"Barely." Niles pulls himself up onto the houseboat's platform and then kneels to tug me up out of the water to sit beside him. He motions to me while I kiss the platform, thanking it for being there when I most needed it. "You fell into the water the first time I met you, and now again today. This is becoming a problem."

I gape at him, water dripping off my nose as I tremble on my forearms and knees. "You're the one causing the problem! If you saw me trying to get onto the houseboat, you could have brought the steps over, so I didn't have to risk falling into the water."

"Where's the fun in that?" Niles helps me slide off my backpack and my shoes, which are now thoroughly drenched. He smirks at me and pats my back while I catch my breath.

I turn over and sit up. I pull my knees to my chest, my chin resting on them while I do my best to steady my breathing. I motion up to Cricket and Honey, who are still on the dock, looking down on me with confusion and worry. Cricket barks, as if asking if she should jump into the water, too.

"You scared them," I tell Niles, trying to block out the

details of his beautiful face. "You scared them, and they're only babies."

Niles quirks his brow at me. "Honey is like, a decade old, which means she is a senior citizen in people years. And Cricket is no pup." When it is clear I am going to lecture him, Niles stands. "Alright, alright. I'll get the dogs." He arranges the ramp on the platform to slant from the houseboat to the dock. "See, it's actually considered rude to come onto a person's houseboat if they don't have the stairs or a ramp up for visitors."

I grumble in response, though I can see his point. "I called out for Jada, but she didn't answer. I was going to leave her a box of cookies."

Niles picks up Honey, who needs coaxing to cross over on the ramp, while Cricket leads the way with full confidence in her strut. "What kind of cookies?"

I glare at him, all turned around, now that I am soaking and completely embarrassed to have fallen into the ocean in front of the hot guy.

Again.

I have dated women. I have dated men. But no one has ever compared to the beauty that is Niles Williams.

It's hard to be haughty when I am dripping and cold, but I manage to raise my nose. "The cookies are for Jada, not you."

Niles sets Honey down on the platform so she can sniff her surroundings. "Hey, I saved your life. I think that gets me at least one cookie."

I narrow an eye at him. "I am this close to pushing you into the water."

Niles laughs and walks to the door, popping it open and inviting me inside. "Jada had to work late. She'll be home soon, though. Here's hoping whatever container you put the cookies in, it's waterproof."

I stand, dripping water all around me. I take out the vacuum-sealed, thankfully waterproof packaging and shove it toward Niles without entering Jada's home for fear of getting water everywhere. "Here. Can you tell Jada I stopped by?" But before I release the box into his grip, I hold it back. "They're for Jada, not you."

Niles gives me a faux pout, his long, curly lashes stealing my breath. "What do I have to do to get a few cookies? Save your life?"

My cheeks heat.

Attractive people like him don't pay attention to me. They certainly don't tease me with a cutesy smile the way Niles is doing.

I try my best to push all attraction out of my mind. "You have to not make me fall into the water in the first place."

He peels off his sopping socks, still standing in the doorway. "How about I give you swimming lessons? I think that's worth at least one cookie."

My mouth pulls to the side. My first instinct is to respond with a childish "I'm not allowed to go swimming," but I know that's not the thing to say. My parents didn't permit me to take lessons, because they worried I would drown (which, given what just happened, I guess they weren't too far off in their paranoia). They never took me to the beach, and I wasn't allowed to go to any parties where there might be a pool. My parents are cautious people, and that trait was passed down to me.

Then again, I did break into City Hall and steal expensive sound equipment, so perhaps I am growing up into a person none of us expected me to become.

Maybe I am a rulebreaker, after all.

I fiddle with the hem of my soaked tank top as I consider Niles' offer. While stealing seemed the thing to do when I had Jada by my side, getting back into the water after I almost just drowned is one step too far for me. "Maybe some other time. I'm not sure. I don't feel like drowning again today."

Plus, there's the obvious fact that he is too beautiful to be near. I would guess swimming lessons might involve us being in close proximity, which isn't a thing I am willing to do with someone this striking.

It's not possible that Niles can read my attraction to him. We are standing several feet apart, and I can barely make eye contact for more than a few seconds before I have to look away.

Niles stands straighter. "Fair enough. The offer doesn't expire, so hit me up when you're tired of drowning."

I weigh his words, wondering when that part of me will

kick in. Maybe that's what Apple Blossom Bay has become for me—a place that won't let me drown.

Dare I say, it's a place where I am encouraged to breathe.

"Thanks," I say to Niles, which isn't something I thought I would utter to the man who scared me so much that I fell into the water—twice, now.

I take my dogs back up the ramp and let my soggy shoes dangle at my side. I take my time making my way home, wondering if I will ever gather enough courage to take Niles up on his offer.

14

PUZZLING OVER ROTTEN FISH

One of the many perks of living in Apple Blossom Bay is that there are all sorts of odd things to do to pass the time. While most people's hobbies seem to center around fishing or various watersports, mine are decidedly less water centric.

The day after I fell in the ocean, I still haven't managed to push Niles' handsome face from my mind, so I figure a good round of puzzling might help me shake my silly crush.

I bring my two dogs to Puzzles and Pins, where I tend to gravitate most often after work. Aside from being a member of their puzzle exchange program, Phyllis told me this morning before work that she and her friends were planning on meeting up here this evening to puzzle together, and they will not forgive me if I don't show up with both dogs.

What can I say? We are a handful of wild women.

Honey and Cricket are greeted by Vivian, who gives them both a dog biscuit from the bowl beside the register and a pat on the head. Though I've interacted with the redheaded owner of this store several times since I moved here, I am surprised when she pulls me in for a hug. Her arms are tight as they squeeze a squeak from me.

"Good to see you, Vivian."

She rocks my body from side to side for a few beats. "I heard the news that you were adopting Honey."

"You did? Word travels fast. I only spoke to Hank's estate lawyer yesterday."

The woman in her sixties smells pleasantly of vanilla perfume, which floods my nose as she prolongs the hug. "That just swells my heart in the best kind of way. Anyone would have jumped at the chance to pamper Cricket, but Honey has a particular way about her. She doesn't like most people. But after seeing the way she clings to you?" Vivian steps back and shakes her head, a soft smile crinkling the corners of her mouth. "I'm glad you two found each other. I'm sure Hank can rest easier, knowing that you are watching over Honey for him."

I lean down and pet both dogs, who lap up the affection. "I'm going to sign some papers to make it all official tomorrow. Can't wait." I kiss Honey's maw and then Cricket's, who stands on her hind legs to garner more attention.

Vivian motions to the small room off to the side of her immaculately clean and well-organized store. "The girls are back there already. Are you staying to puzzle, or did you stop by to exchange for a new one?"

I motion to the room dedicated to puzzlers only. "I'm meeting up with the girls. It was good to see you." I turn and trot toward the room at the back of the store. There is a clear vibe of "do not enter unless you are a puzzle fanatic." It feels like I am entering hallowed grounds.

I love it here. I love that these senior citizen women have accepted me into their fold. I love that Vivian referred to them as "the girls". The whole thing makes me feel as if I have lived here for years, and I fit in seamlessly with the cool crowd.

I've never fit in anywhere, but I've found my people here.

The moment I enter, I am greeted with hugs, kisses on the cheek, and peanut brittle, which Phyllis made from scratch.

The backroom has high-traffic carpeting and a large round table in the center with a puzzle scattered across the top in pieces. There's a long, thin table pushed up against the wall for the refreshments we are allowed to bring in.

I take a bite of Phyllis' peanut brittle, my eyes immediately rolling back with delight. "Teach me how to make this? Usually peanut brittle sticks to my teeth like concrete. But yours is heavenly."

Phyllis takes off her knitted pearl-colored sweater and drapes it over the chair. "Absolutely. Oo! What did you bring us?" She is wearing a peach summer dress with plenty of lace around the shin-length hem. The capped sleeves cup her shoulders. She looks fresh out of an old musical, and completely like herself.

I love it.

Quite the contrast from my jeans and gray t-shirt.

I cling to a box of chocolates I bought from the grocery store to share with the girls, because puzzles are best enjoyed with friends and food, I am learning.

Edna claps her bony hands together, her wiry smile broadening across her face. "The gang's all here! Let's get cracking on this thing." Her hands go straight from petting Cricket to sifting through the scattered puzzle pieces that have been strewn across the round table.

Lorraine's light brown hair is done in a fancy knot, her attire breezy. She is always a blend of stylish and informal. I often wonder if she ran a company or something before moving here. She looks put together in that effortless way, wearing clothes with such confidence that nothing would dare spill on them. "I have been dying to see you ladies. You won't believe the dream I had last night. Hank joined our puzzle time, wearing one of your dresses, Phyllis. The seafoam green one."

Phyllis chortles at Lorraine's dream while Edna whistles appreciatively.

I'll admit, my visuals of Hank are limited, but that is a good one.

I chuckle as I set down the box of chocolates beside the peanut brittle so I can untether the dogs from their leashes. They are well behaved and can roam freely through the backroom without incident.

For five solid minutes, the four of us are quiet while we search for corner pieces and then sides. "I can't shake the sight of Hank," I admit, breaking the silence. "I want to figure out who killed him, but I keep coming up empty."

Phyllis shakes her head as she studies the lid of the thousand-piece puzzle. "It's his kids. It's always the kids when it's someone of a certain age. They don't want to visit us, but they want our toys once we die. It's awful."

My stomach churns at the bitter statement that might very well prove true. "I hope that's not it." My fingers flutter over the mess of pieces, turning over the ones that are wrong-side-up, so we can see what we're working with. "I ran into Bradley and Hattie at the dock yesterday. They were with the lawyer, arguing over who gets to keep Hank's boat. Seemed kind of intense."

Lorraine is taller than most, her attitude flaring as she locates a coveted pink edge piece. "That boat and this dog were Hank's favorite parts of life," she declares, pointing at Honey. "To think of those two only showing up here to fight over the boat? Give me a break. Neither of them can afford the time or upkeep of a boat like Hank's. He kept that thing immaculate."

Edna locates a few more edge pieces, making a pile of pink-colored ones to see if they fit together. "Hank used to take neighborhood kids out on the water during the summer and teach the more rascally ones how to fish," she explains to me. "A sweeter soul I've never known. Even tolerated those wild Dunphy boys, God bless him."

A gentle smile finds my face. "See, this is what I needed. To come here and listen to stories that warm my heart. Hearing Hank's kids bicker about the boat left a sour taste in my insides."

Edna chuckles, her bejeweled fingers reaching across the table. "I can imagine. No, no. After he retired from the fishing trade, Hank used that boat to help the kids more than anything else. He was always taking them out on the water to give the young mothers around here a break for a few hours. It's hard to be wild or irritating when you've got nothing but the water, Hank and Honey. Didn't say much. Had that peaceful way about him that a person gets when the water is their home."

Edna's words make me think of Jada's houseboat, and how tranquil life lived on the water must be. "I like the way you put that, Edna. That's a pretty thought—the water being a person's home."

"Oh, sure. A trip out on the water with Hank usually would set just about any wrong right." Edna fits two pieces together, holding up our very first triumph, to which we all clap. She sets it down on the table, her eyes searching for more pink edge pieces. "The last person he ever took out on the ocean was Wally." She points to me. "The boy who had your job before you moved here, Hannah."

My expression falls. "Poor thing. I don't know much about Wally."

Lorraine's wry expression speaks volumes. "He was fired from the grocery store, which is a hard feat to accomplish. Larry is pretty mellow."

Edna fills in the blanks for me. "Larry left Wall Street to come here. Burnt out on the greed of it all, I guess. Took over the general store and turned it into the Forgotten Stock Market we have now."

Lorraine nods. "Larry is one of us now. Laid back, valuing a person's quality of life rather than just their usefulness. You have to work real hard to get fired around here. Most of us don't get too worked up about the details."

"That's a shame the job didn't work out for Wally," I offer. "I really love stocking shelves. I didn't realize how much I would enjoy it until I started up here. Larry lets me bring the dogs to work. It's so peaceful."

Lorraine nods. "Most of the jobs here are. Wally stole money from the register, so Larry had to let him go." She shakes her head. "It's no real surprise. Wally was supposed to clean my gutters two weeks ago. He got up on the ladder and made a big stink about how much work there was to do. I went out to the store while he was working, and when I came home, he told me he was done. I paid him, and I thought that was that. Wouldn't you know that when it rained next, my gutters were still just as clogged."

Phyllis clucks her tongue. "Wally was sent here by his parents when he got kicked out of school. He lives with his uncle, who has a place just outside of Apple Blossom Bay. Now that Wally doesn't work at the grocery store, I don't see him as much. It's just as well. He was a terrible stock boy."

Though I know I'm going off-topic, I can't help my train of thought that runs off the tracks on occasion. "I got a bachelor's degree in business, all to find that the job that suits me best is stocking shelves." I shake my head at myself. "I wish I hadn't wasted so much time and money."

Phyllis wraps an arm around me while we examine the puzzle pieces strewn about. She squeezes my bicep to bolster me. "You landed here at just the right time in your life. Best not look back and criticize the steps we took to get here. It's better to be grateful for the path that led us to this place. To this puzzle." She kisses my cheek. "To each other."

I lean into the affection, deciding to take her wisdom and bury it in my heart. "Regrets don't help much, do they."

"Not the tiniest bit."

The four of us work in semi-silence, muttering about searching for a particular piece while the stress of life begins to release its stranglehold on each of us. I notice my own shoulders loosening while the other women begin to relax, as well.

This place is magical; I am convinced.

Lorraine keeps her eyes on the pieces when she speaks. "I guess Dave is a shoo-in for the fish-off next month, now that Hank is gone."

Phyllis nods her head, but I speak up. "Fish-off? What's that?"

"A fishing competition that happens every year. It's only for residents of Apple Blossom Bay. There are loads of fishing competitions that happen here all the time, but this one is smaller, and the people here get much more into the sport of it. Hank's won three years in a row. You know that irked Dave."

The name rings in my memory. "Dave is the fourth at the poker night with Hank, Paul and Larry, right?"

Lorraine nods. "Correct. Maybe Dave's got a chance this year, now that Hank's..." She swallows hard. "Well, you know."

"Is Dave a competitive fisher?" I inquire, not knowing much about the people here yet.

Edna laughs—a wry sound escaping her thin, pink-painted lips. "You could say that. You could also say he's competitive about everything and is also a sore loser, which is a bad combination. You should have seen the photos of Hank, Dave, and Melinda—first, second and third place last year. Two grins hemmed in with the sourest frown I've ever seen on a grown man." Edna chuckles at the memory after she imitates Dave's moping. "Dave will be gunning for first place, now that Hank is gone."

"What's the prize for first place?"

Lorraine quirks her brow at me. "Why? Do you fish?"

I snort at the notion. "No. I don't even know how to

swim. I like my feet on solid ground. I was asking because I wanted to know if the prize for first place is worth killing a man over."

The three women stop moving, gaping at me as if I've said something off-color.

Finally, Phyllis replies. "I don't know how Hank died, but I can't imagine Dave would kill a man over a year's supply of fish fry from the Rotten Fish."

I blanch. "Is that the name of an actual restaurant here?"

The three nod in reverence. "Best fish fry in the world, if you ask me," says Phyllis.

My head tilts to the side. "That's first place? No prize money?"

Phyllis shakes her head. "Most people around here don't hop too high for money. It's the simple pleasures that are worth the struggle. The Rotten Fish has the best fish fry in the state, and the awards to back it up. Having an unlimited supply is a nice prize, but it's the bragging rights and the sport of it all that draws people in. You even get your picture on the wall of their restaurant. If the people around here cared about the money, they'd compete in one of the many other fishing competitions that are held here throughout the summer. Those are open to anyone with a fishing license."

I nod, absorbing the nuances that make this town unique.

So, Hank didn't join the competition for the money,

just for the fish fry and bragging rights. Dave, as well. I'm not sure unlimited fish fry or pride are worth killing a man over, but until I do a little more digging, I won't know for sure that Dave is not responsible for murdering his friend in cold blood.

15

SECOND PLACE

I like walking the dogs. I haven't had this much exercise in my life, and I love every second of it. When the puzzle gals told me Dave would be on the water fishing before my shift started at the grocery store the next morning, I knew a beachfront walk would be how I should start my day.

Edna's instructions were simple enough. I'm to look for a boat called Erma's Heart. Though, this time of the morning just before the sun rises, there are dozens of boats missing from the harbor. I guess dawn is the best time to go fishing.

I can't say fishing has ever appealed to me, but now that I am walking barefoot through the sand before the world has properly awoken, I can see why the calm of the waters could lure people out when they might otherwise be sleeping.

I like the sound of the waves lapping at the shore, and so do the dogs. I take off their leashes and let them run freely. The two rascals get their paws wet as they egg each other on to roll in the damp sand. I love how happy Cricket and Honey are together. They are sweethearts, with Honey giving gentle barks when Cricket gets wild in her happiness and wanders too far.

I want to be like that. My precious Pomeranian has a spirit of adventure I never possessed. Though, maybe I can't say that anymore. I am currently out before the sun is up, hunting down a murder suspect so I can cross him off my list.

Maybe I am braver than I thought.

My toes bunch in the sand when I pick a spot on the beach and sit down so I can watch the sunrise. I am supposed to be searching for a boat called Erma's Heart, but I can't ignore the pinkish orange streaks that are beginning to paint themselves in the sky along the water-lined horizon.

It's quiet out here, which gives my mind time to unwind.

I didn't have many friends or interests back home. If I wanted to try something new, there were plenty of reasons not to go out on a limb. That's how you fall, after all.

But here, Aunt Em encourages me to take risks. She doesn't care if my dog biscuits don't turn out, which means I can experiment with ingredients I otherwise wouldn't try, for fear of failing.

Gratitude wells up in me for the gift that is being allowed to be imperfect. I don't have all the answers to life's questions, nor do I need them in this moment.

My toes bury deeper in the sand as a light breeze brushes over my arms. I watch the sun peak over the horizon, greeting me with its welcoming smile, as if I belong here.

I've never belonged anywhere before this.

My dogs bound to me, lapping at my face to thank me for the early morning adventure. I giggle as they tackle me backwards with their affection, kissing me again and again until I have to roll over so I can wipe my wet face on my arm.

When they return to the shore, they bark at a boat that is sailing back to the dock.

Sure enough, the words "Erma's Heart" are painted in blue on the side of the white boat. Leave it to my dogs to find the thing I'm searching for while I lose focus looking at nature.

I stand, giving my attention to the dock, suddenly unsure what the plan was in coming here. I'm no good at breaking the ice. I never mastered small talk or really any kind of conversational gymnastics.

Still, I breathe in the ocean air and march to the shore with my head up, as if I have all the confidence in the world, even if I don't possess the right words.

I wait on the shore, not venturing to the dock because, after falling into the water the other day, I still don't have my sea legs. The dogs run happily through the sand while I watch Dave dock his boat, tie it up and cut the engine.

The man emerging is shorter than I am. He carries a cooler that looks like it has seen better days, if the grime on the outside is any indication. He bobs his head at me—the only other person around. "Morning."

"It's peaceful out, isn't it?" I offer. "I'm Hannah Hart, Emily's niece."

Dave sets down his cooler. "Ah. I heard about you. Em couldn't stop talking about how excited she was to have her favorite niece come to stay with her for the summer. I'm Dave. Nice to meet you, Hannah Hart." He offers to shake my hand, but then pulls it back because I'm guessing his hands are less than clean.

"Likewise." I motion to his cooler. "Did you catch anything this morning?"

Dave nods, grinning at me. "Sure did." He pops open the lid to show me the very dead fish. "Caught me some dinner. I always fish better when it's not a competition. I wish I did this well under pressure. I think the fish can smell the desperation on me when I'm trying too hard. But this morning, the ocean was just right."

I tilt my head at him. "Competition?"

Dave wipes his hands off on a bandana that he pulls from the pocket of his cargo shorts. "There's a local fish-off here. It's for residents of Apple Blossom Bay only, so it's more for pride than the prize. Still, I worry the fish will turn on me because I want to win. Do you fish?"

"Only for compliments," I quip. "Who's the big contender this year for the local fish-off?"

Dave lowers his chin. "I suppose I am. I've come in second place a few years in a row. My buddy Hank was always number one, but he passed recently. It's not as fun to win when the competition doesn't keep you on your toes."

"But you've got a better chance at first place, now, don't you? That's nice."

Dave shrugs. "Sure, but without Hank, it's not the same. I'll still compete just because it's a town event. But if I win, that trophy is going straight on Hank's grave, because I know if he was alive, he would've beat me."

My heart tugs in my chest. "I think that's sweet, considering Hank the winner. You don't seem sour about getting beaten by Hank last year. That's nice."

Dave chuckles. "So long as I catch something worth bragging about, I'm happy. The winner gets unlimited fish fry for the year. Every year that Hank came in first, he would have me over the next day, and we would eat ourselves sick using the fish fry he'd won." He hoists up the cooler once again. "Like I said, it's not about the prize. It won't be the same out there without Hank this year. If I win, I won't be able to have my friend over for fish fry. Makes the prize a little less sweet."

"It was nice to meet you, Dave. I'm sorry you lost your friend."

"Thank you, Hannah Grapefruit." When I gape that he

knows my nickname, he snickers at me. "That's right, Emily talks. She's been telling us every story she knows about you for months." He nods toward Honey. "You taking care of Hank's dog for him?"

I nod happily. "Sure am. Hank's lawyer said I get to keep Honey, so she can stay with her friends here."

Dave smirks at me. "I'm sure Hank wouldn't have it any other way. If Honey ever wants to go out on the boat with me, let me know and I'll take her. She and Hank used to go out on the water all the time."

"Thanks." Though, I know I will never take Dave up on that offer. Just going on Jada's houseboat is the most risk I am willing to try, and I've fallen into the ocean twice already.

Dave waddles off with his cooler, while I watch my dogs run after each other.

No, Dave didn't kill Hank. He didn't have the motive. While I'm sure one could fake sadness easily enough, I didn't get that feeling from him. He seems genuinely sad to have lost his friend and fishing buddy.

But if Dave didn't kill Hank, then who did?

16

JADA MACKEREL

When the door to Jada's houseboat opens after I say goodbye to Dave, I perk up, waving her down. The sun is still rising, highlighting my movements just enough for her to see me flagging her attention.

Jada grins at me and trots in my direction with her backpack over her shoulders. "Good morning, bestie."

I smile at the greeting because it's just about the greatest one a girl can get. "Good morning yourself, bestie. You off to work?"

Jada's head bobs. "I've got a display to finish up in the hallway before school starts, so I need to get cracking on it."

"Do you need help? My shift doesn't start for another hour."

Jada's brow quirks. "And you just so happened to be hanging around the shore for no reason?"

I motion to Dave, who is far enough away from us that he can't overhear. "I was crossing a suspect off the list."

Jada and I trot to the grass. The dogs follow behind while they enjoy their own little conversation of snorts and whines. I love that they have each other.

Jada has several rolls of colored paper sticking out of her backpack, bobbing along with plenty of pep in her step. Her box braids with pink thread running through them are pulled back with a yellow ribbon, showing off her large eyes and pretty smile. "It's draw your favorite fish week," Jada explains. "My kindergarteners are drawing their fish, practicing their cutting skills to cut them out, and then they're going to tape them to the board in the hallway so their art can be on display." She motions to herself. "I don't want to call myself a creative genius, but if you're not, then I guess I'll have to pick up the megaphone and announce it to the world myself."

I cast her an adoring look. "You're a creative genius if I've ever seen one." My arms swing at my sides while we walk in tandem. "Seriously, though. That's very cool."

"My fish is a Jada mackerel. She swims at top speed and never needs caffeine to keep active, but she caffeinates on the weekends just to live on the edge. She has pink scales, and she gives fantastic fin high-fives."

I snicker at the nature of the project. "That is creative. I suppose my fish would be just figuring out how to navigate the waters. But she's got two little fish by her side, and tends to swim near the Jada mackerel, so I think she'll find her way eventually."

Jada bumps her hip to mine. "I know she will. Stick by the water, and you won't stay lost for long." She rolls her eyes. "I know that's such an Apple Blossom Bay thing to say, but it never stops being true. The water figures you out when you're not sure who you want to be."

I take in her wisdom and mull it over while we walk.

When we reach her school, I can't help the sweet coo that escapes me once we go into the building and round the hallways that lead to her classroom. "Oh, look at the little cubbies! They're so small and cute. And look at the nametags you made. My gosh, you *are* a creative genius. That's adorable!" I point to the fish-themed nametags over each cubby. Each one has bubbles coming out of the fish's mouth to form the child's name in rounded letters.

Jada touches one of the nametags. "This is Anthony's cubby. He draws pictures of all the dogs in town. Totally precious."

My whole being lights up. "Has he done one of Honey?"

"Not recently. But when he does, I'll snap a photo and send it to you."

Everything in her room has an Under the Sea design to it. There are blue streamers hanging down from the ceiling, along with plastic clear round bowls with fake fish suspended inside. There is a huge plush shark in the corner of the room with a giant toothbrush in his fin, reminding the children to brush each of their teeth every day if they want to keep them healthy.

I mean, totally precious.

We take out her supplies and then head back into the hallway. I make myself useful spreading out the light blue paper over the corkboard, while Jada tacks it into place.

"I don't know how you were planning on doing this by yourself," I comment as I unroll the border paper and begin stapling it to the outer edges once the blue is in place.

Jada shrugs. "It always manages to come together one way or another. I usually can guilt my brother into helping me out, but Niles was being annoying last night, so he's getting some much-needed space."

I know my cheeks are heating at mention of Jada's handsome older brother, so I turn my head away when I speak. "I'm glad I happened to be in the area. I was there to talk with Dave, who couldn't be nicer. I'm starting to think a ghost killed Hank, because no one in Apple Blossom Bay has motive to be terrible."

Jada snickers. "You thought Dave was the killer? I could have saved you the trouble there. Dave is a good guy. A little intense about odd things, but not competitive enough to murder."

I search through the craft supplies. "I figured that out this morning. Pass me that extra roll of border paper?"

Jada gives me the roll and then starts in on the creative

work, for which I have little aptitude. "My money's on Paul. I mean, I'm hoping it's a ghost because I like Paul, but he lost big in the poker game with Larry, Hank and Dave. Didn't Larry mention that Paul wanted Hank to throw in the deed to his boat? That's motive right there."

My head bobs. "Sure, but Hank folded, so there wasn't the chance of winning Hank's boat."

Jada pins a cutout of a giant fishbowl in the center of the board. "Maybe Paul was sore about that. Maybe he really wanted Hank's boat, and when Hank didn't put it up for collateral, Paul got all mad about it."

I staple the border along the left side. "Wouldn't he be clambering to take the boat now, then? So far, it's only Hank's children who seem to care enough about the boat to fight in front of the lawyer for it."

"True. And Paul didn't win the pot at their poker night; Larry did. So Paul wouldn't have gotten the boat anyway, even if Hank had put it in the deed." She tilts her head to the side while she takes out a permanent marker. "Still, it sounds like a decent reason to murder to me. Sour grapes over not winning the boat or the money. Knowing the boat is probably going to family has to sting."

I chuckle at her reasoning. "You sure want Paul to be guilty, don't you."

Jada's neck shrinks. "I miscalculated my checking account last week, over-drafted and got charged a fee. I blame Paul, because obviously it's not my fault I miscalculated."

"Obviously." I tilt my head sympathetically. "I hate it when I do that."

"It would be convenient if Paul was the killer, because then everything could be his fault, including my over-draft fee."

"Solid logic. But killing Hank wouldn't get Paul the boat, if that's what he wanted. Hank's kids get to fight over their father's things."

Jada harrumphs. "Oh, fine. But then our most likely suspect really is a ghost, which I'm guessing doesn't help much. Deputy Hanson can't exactly slap handcuffs on a ghost. The cuffs would go straight through."

"Boo," I complain.

Jada's hip juts to the side. "Then again, there's the mysterious lawncare person who came to Hank's neighbor, and whom Hank let into his house. Maybe there's something there."

"Is it really so strange to have solicitors?"

Jada's shoulders deflate. "Not really."

"If anyone, I think Mrs. Finch has it in her to hurt Hank. She was about to spray Honey in the face. She cares more about her petunias than she does people."

I'm still stewing about that.

Jada weighs my words. "She's a definite suspect, that's for sure."

I step back from the board, wishing things could be simpler. "Okay, enough of that for now. I'm spinning myself in circles. What comes next?"

"The fish, but not yet. I have to glue on the bubbles."

"Huh?"

"You'll see. It can't be a boring 2-D display, Hannah. It needs to be an actual beautiful work of art. It has to be interesting. You know I can't do things halfway."

I blink at her. "You think I know the first thing about beautiful works of art?"

Jada waves off my confusion. "You know that things need to look a certain way because of how meticulous you are about stocking the shelves at the grocery store. Larry was bragging about you yesterday to Em. Said you were the best hire he's made since Betty. You know that the things on the shelf have to be appealing, or people won't find what they need. Same thing here. The display needs to be eye-catching, or the kids won't care that it exists. It will become white noise in their vision, which is the opposite of what we're trying to accomplish here."

My hand goes over my heart. "Larry was saying nice things about me to Aunt Em?"

Jada nods while she pins a string in place. "Sure was."

Sweetness coats my insides while I help Jada position four-inch plastic bubbles around the display. Honey and Cricket wag their tails, sniffing the various decorations while we work. They have a long range, since it's only us in this part of the school. They need to investigate every inch of the floor, occasionally yipping to the other if they've discovered something of note.

Jada reaches down to pet Cricket. "I love these dogs

together. Honey is so much better with a buddy. She's like, one whole foot away from you. That's gotta mean she's relaxing." She kneels and kisses Cricket's maw. "I think Cricket's just got that way about her. She can charm anybody, even an introvert like Honey."

I smile at my dogs. "I sign the papers from the lawyer after work today. I can't wait to make it official. I'm going to bake more dog biscuits tonight to celebrate."

Jada lights up. "Oo! Do you need help?"

I bump my hip to hers. "I can't possibly survive without it."

"Deal. I'll swing by this evening, then. I want Em to teach me how to make shrimp and grits." She holds up her hands to stave off my warning. "I know, I know. But with Em's help, I finally mastered mashed potatoes. I think I'm ready to step up my game. You make the dog food; I'll make the people food."

Jada's mashed potatoes were certainly edible.

That is the best compliment I can give them.

At my look of hesitation, she harrumphs. "I'll order us a pizza if it turns out terrible."

I snicker at her plan. "Sounds good."

I never had a close friend who looked for any excuse to spend time with me, but I find that the more often I spend days with Jada, the happier I become.

While I'm not sure I will get to the bottom of who killed poor Hank, I am grateful that I am learning how to make friends.

17

WALL TO WALL

Stocking shelves might not be everyone's idea of happiness, and I'm not even sure that's the only reason I am smiling through work today. Really, it's that I got to hang out with Jada this morning before work, and now I get to be with my two dogs all day long. I think they could make any job the best occupation ever, simply by being cute and wagging their sweet little tails.

But today is especially wonderful because I get to adopt Honey after my shift.

Everyone gets a smile from me, even if I don't know them and they are clearly only here to get what they need from the store and go. The dogs are bathed in kisses from me and the occasional treat from the shoppers who filter in and out. I was never this engaged when I worked at the gas station. I rarely made eye contact unless I was being yelled at if a person's credit card wouldn't go through, and they blamed me for it. But at the Forgotten Stock Market, I go out of my way to smile at people and ask them if they need help.

I barely recognize myself.

My mind keeps pinging back to Hank. Even though I never met the man, I want to do right by his dog. It is clear that he loved Honey very much, so today is important. It feels like he is passing something precious onto me.

I also really want to make sure that no one is coming after Honey.

I mull over Mrs. Finch's attitude toward my sweet dog. Readying to spray a dog in the face over a few flowers? I have some strong opinions about a person willing to do that.

Part of my job is going to the checkout and taking the discarded items that people thought they wanted to purchase, but then changed their minds at the checkout. I take those goods and reshelve them, which gives me the opportunity to chat with the friendliest woman in the world: Betty.

I love her energy. Betty has a hug for me every time she sees my face, which is several times every workday. She also has a treat for my dogs tucked in her red store apron. I'm guessing that is most likely the reason why they are so well behaved for her.

"Sit, little lovelies," Betty commands in her caring coo.

Honey and Cricket obey easily, because they are good dogs, but also because they know who holds the treats.

They munch while I collect the castoff items. "How's your day going so far, Betty?"

She punches a few keys on her register. "Oh, can't complain. But if I could, I would complain that those dogs always stay right near you, and they hardly ever come to visit me. Don't they know that I need a little love, too?"

I chuckle at what Betty considers a complaint. "I'll remind them to beg for treats more often."

My vision snags on a man in cut-offs, standing near the exit with his shopping bag in his hand. He tears off a slip of paper from the "Local Yokels" board designated for local companies to advertise their services to the shoppers.

When he leaves, I meander over to the board, wondering if I should be looking for a dog sitter, in the rare chance I might need that kind of thing. This seems to be the place where one might advertise their dog sitting services.

But when I look at the various items for sale and services offered, there are no dog sitters listed.

There is one thing that does catch my eye, though. Mrs. Finch mentioned there was a lawncare service where the man was dressed in a yellow shirt who came to her door. "Wall to Wall Lawncare" has a flyer with their logo on it, which is yellow, along with a picture of an employee, whose uniform is a cheery canary color.

I gnaw on my lower lip when I recall Mrs. Finch saying that she didn't even answer the door to the solicitor, but

Hank did. Hank went so far as to let the man into his house, she told me.

It's then that a new thought occurs to me.

Why would a lawncare person need to come *inside* a person's house? Their entire job is the outside of a home, not indoors.

I shift my weight from one foot to the other as I pull my phone out and take a picture of the flyer, so I can ask Mrs. Finch later if this was the company she saw.

Maybe an employee working for Wall to Wall Lawncare saw something that might be helpful in finding Hank's killer.

When my shift ends, I practically skip out of the grocery store, putting the flyer out of my mind because I have somewhere important to be.

Honey is about to get a new mommy. I don't want to be late to signing the papers that will make this sweet dog forever mine.

18

DOG ADOPTION

My call to the lawncare company is short since their answering machine picks up. It might be nice to hire them to do some work for Aunt Em in the yard. While they are over, I can ask if they visited Hank. Then I can see if they found anything abnormal in his house when they were there giving him a quote.

Em doesn't need help with her flowers, but she might appreciate a company dealing with the lawn, so she doesn't have to. Now that I'm getting a paycheck, I want to chip in and make her life easier.

By the time I drive myself and my dogs to the lawyer's office, I am practically bouncing in my seat. I kiss both my dogs and then fix their leashes in place on my belt loop. I lead them into the lawyer's office once I see the sign that reads "Leashed Dogs Welcome".

Only in Apple Blossom Bay.

I greet the receptionist with a smile and wait until I am called back to sign whatever papers need to be dealt with. "Thanks for making this happen so quickly for me," I offer when I take the seat across from Javier at his desk. "Honey is just the best. I'm glad I get to be her mom officially."

The lawyer gives me a wry look as he takes out a folder. "You really love that corgi, don't you."

"Who wouldn't? She's a sweetheart, and she gets along great with Cricket, who sometimes needs an older sister to keep her grounded."

As if on cue, Cricket stands on her hind legs, her front paws on the side of my chair. I lift her up and hold her like a baby, rocking her while I stroke her belly.

This dog has a very good life.

And because of her, now so do I.

Honey sniffs the office's corners, and then settles atop my feet, warming them just in case I need it.

My gosh, I never dreamed I would get this lucky.

Javier chuckles as he slides the transfer of ownership papers over to me. "And you can take care of Honey? You can feed her and put a roof over her head?"

"Of course. I know Hank fed her the good stuff, so that's what she has with me, too. I don't want her to have to change food. She's been through enough, what with losing Hank. The whole thing is just awful."

The lawyer nods, as if that's what he was hoping to hear. "The real prize seems to be Hank's boat. His kids have been fighting over it all week."

I shrug. "I'm not much of a water person." I kiss Cricket's maw. "I'm more of a dog person."

Javier chuckles at our affectionate display. "Clearly."

"I hope his kids work it out. I'm just happy I get to snuggle the dog. I didn't know Hank, so I realize how lucky I am that Honey took to me so well." I lower my voice to a whisper in hopes that Honey doesn't overhear as I lean forward. "I'm secretly grateful his kids didn't want Honey. I love being with her."

The lawyer watches me sign the papers, then he makes me a copy and hands me the duplicate. "Well, that's good for my soul. I hate it when people fight over things and forget the living beings in the mix. Hank was a good man. He loved Honey even more than he loved that boat, which is saying something. He had very particular instructions concerning Honey."

My phone rings in my pocket. When I check the caller ID, I see that it is the lawncare service I left a message for earlier. "Thanks for helping me with this," I offer to the lawyer as I stand, assuming the meeting is over now that I have ownership of Honey.

Javier holds up his hand like he means to say something more, but I answer my call before he can make himself heard. "Hello?" I say on the phone as I wave an apologetic goodbye to the lawyer.

"Wall to Wall Lawncare. I just got your message, saying you were looking for a lawncare service."

"Sure am." I click my fingers to my dogs, who follow

me out of the building and into the sunshine with plenty of slack on their leashes. I give the man my information, telling him the address and what I need done for Aunt Em.

It's nice to be able to pitch in around the house. I hated the first few weeks spent being a sponge. Now I can do something nice for Aunt Em, who welcomed me into her home so joyfully.

The company can meet me at the house tomorrow, which works well for me.

My dogs waste no time getting into the car, wagging their tails and circling each other before they land on Honey lying on the floor and Cricket panting happily on the passenger's seat. I call Aunt Em on the way, telling her the good news.

"I was thinking of baking more dog biscuits to celebrate," I tell my aunt. "And Jada wants you to teach her how to make shrimp and grits."

Em laughs. "Done. Come on home, Hannah Grapefruit. I want to hug our new family member!"

19

DOG PARADE

The air feels crisp with possibility as joy floods my system when I end the call with my aunt. This is how life should be. Hank can rest peacefully, now that his dog will be lovingly cared for.

I whistle the entire way to the house, overjoyed that Honey is officially mine. I did this. I made this choice to do something good for myself, and the world opened up, as if me wanting to be happy is not unreasonable in the least.

I love the spring air. It is laced with flowers and freshly mown grass. Everything feels new and beautiful, and I couldn't be more grateful.

My dogs hop out of the car when we get home. Cricket leads the way, scampering up the driveway to the house. Honey stays at my heels because I am her safe place.

I love that she trusts me, and vow silently to make good

on her assumptions that I am a quality person on which she can rely.

When I get to the front door, it bursts open with a lively "Congratulations!" belting out from my aunt and several others, who wear party hats and blow on kazoos.

I startle, jumping back until I put it together that my aunt gathered up our friends for a celebration. My hand flies over my chest when I see a banner stretched across the living room that reads, "Welcome Home, Honey and Cricket".

I gasp at the display, taking in the women around me who are all jumping up and down with grins on their faces. Their advanced ages don't slow their exuberance in the least.

I blink as I stumble backwards. "You all came over to dote on Honey and Cricket?"

Jada throws her arms around me. "You didn't think we would let you celebrate by making biscuits, did you?"

Aunt Em straightens her party hat. "I realized I didn't throw Cricket a 'Welcome to the Family' party yet, so it's for the both of them." She bows to the furry guests of honor. "Forgive my oversight, my princesses."

Cricket yips while Honey clings to my ankles.

My friends are here, which isn't the true shock. The surprise is that *I have friends*. Lots of them, and they all came to celebrate my dogs.

Lorraine, Edna, Phyllis, Dorothy, Betty, Vivian, Em and

Jada take turns kissing my cheeks and lavishing the dogs with love.

Phyllis pets Honey while Lorraine lifts Cricket to give her a kiss and a cuddle. Lorraine's face sours when Cricket gets carried away and licks her teeth. "Oh, goodness. I guess I forgot to floss this morning. Thanks, Cricket!"

Betty claps her hands, turning in a circle to garner the dogs' attention. "We're going on a celebration walk through the city, since it's Honey's first official day with her new family. We've got the route all mapped out. We're celebrating!"

Jada places a party hat atop my head, dancing out the front door. When the women file out behind her, Dorothy hands out sashes that read "Dog Parade".

They actually planned this out. Flabbergast steals any words that might come forth as Dorothy drapes a silk sash over my shoulder and tugs the end to my opposite hip.

I gape at Dorothy. "Did you have these made?"

Dorothy shakes her head. "Borrowed from the last time there was a dog adoption in town. We didn't go all out for Cricket, since she's not new here, and only changed addresses. But like Em said; that was our oversight. Cricket deserves a true Apple Blossom Bay celebration, just like Honey."

I'm barely keeping up.

My aunt grins at me. "We do this every time someone gets a new dog around here. It's a good way for the dog to get acquainted with the town. We didn't do it with Cricket yet, so this is a celebration for Honey *and* Cricket. They have a lot to celebrate, and the whole town is ready for it."

I nearly choke on my reply. "The whole town?"

Phyllis nods, twirling in a circle so her red velvet dress flares out at the hips. "Dog parades are my favorite kind. Get some clothes on those dogs, and let's go!"

I can barely keep up with my eccentric aunt and her goofy friends (who are becoming my friends, too).

Jada whips out a flowered cape for Honey, attaching it to her collar. Aunt Em slips a pink tutu over Cricket's head and belly, because there is nothing cuter than a fluffy dog in a tutu.

Phyllis frowns at me as I stand on the front porch. "You can't go out like that." She motions to my jeans and gray t-shirt shirt.

I glance down at my attire. "What's wrong with what I'm wearing?"

Phyllis tsks me. "There's no glitter. There's no ruffles. You don't even have any bells on your clothes. How will people know you're celebrating?"

I snicker at her apparent issue with my wardrobe. "I don't own anything like that, so this is as good as it gets, Phyllis." I motion to my torso. "Look, there aren't any stains on my shirt. That's a step up for me."

"Not on my watch!" Aunt Em chimes in, brandishing a purple hat that has lavender and pink tulle streaming out from the back. The material stretches down to my ankles and is laden with silver sparkles.

If ever there was a more ridiculously lavish hat, I do not know it.

Aunt Em kisses my cheek. "Perfect! Now you look like a dog owner."

I laugh aloud, relishing the sound of my joy when it hits the air.

I skip off the porch back out into the evening sunshine, the tulle sparkling behind me. If this is life in a small town, I didn't know the joy I was missing. Now that I have a taste of the good stuff, I'm not sure I can ever go back to my quiet ways.

I was made for dog parades.

And glittery hats with trains, apparently.

The women are dressed in show-stopping outfits meant to catch the eye. It's like they are each their own parade float, trussed up to bring joy to any onlookers who might be in need of some cheer.

Aunt Em leads the way, pulling out a baton with a toy dog fixed on the end. She throws her head back and marches with her knees up high, her purple flowery ankle-length dress flowing without apology. She parades us down the street and turns onto the main road that leads to the lake. She grins the entire way, so we have no choice but to enjoy the goofiness along with her.

Jada's phone plays a joyful Sousa march, blasted loud enough for anyone nearby to stop and stare.

Phyllis has a pocket filled with glitter, which she throws into the air in celebration.

My inner introvert starts to come back to life when we turn onto the main road, but it seems that this is not an uncommon occurrence around here, because no one is scratching their head in our direction. They seem to collectively agree that this is normal, and a perfect way to spend an evening. Cricket prances happily, strutting to show off her cute outfit to the people on the street.

Aunt Em must have put in calls to the entire town, because it seems they have all come out to greet my dogs and welcome them to their new family.

My eyes well up with pride as a few children run out with dog bones in their small fists. "It's the dog parade!" One of them shouts excitedly.

What a childhood this is for them, throwing a parade for two precious dogs.

Maybe I didn't understand the important things in life before I came here but watching old men and young children gush for my dogs while the women clap along to Jada's music, I know my priorities have been set right.

It is the most natural thing in the world for this town to celebrate the adoption of a dog. We all wave to the onlookers, showing off our lavish attire with pride. My "Dog Parade" sash glitters as if the sun itself has shown up to strut with us on this special day.

Honey and Cricket accept each bone, each treat, and each stroke of their fur with confusion and joy.

We're all going to sleep well tonight.

We march by the coffee kiosk, the fish market, Puzzles

and Pins (which is closed, since Vivian is marching with us. She hung a sign on the door that reads "Closed for Dog Parade" like the cutie she is), the bed and breakfast, the clock store, and many more. Each owner comes out with their patrons and claps for my dogs. Even the people who are clearly tourists here for the ocean come out to join in the goofy traditions that make this town special.

Children dance in the parade behind us, waving to the onlookers as if this is the most important day of their lives.

I love everything about this town. I can't believe my good fortune that fate landed me here with these incredible women and these beautiful dogs.

20

BENTLEY'S OCEAN POTIONS

*S*leeping with two dogs in my bed and the windows open all night is just about the best feeling in the world. I love the breeze that wakes me, and the dog kisses that coax me to stretch and finally sit up.

Cricket climbs on my lap and rolls onto her back, knowing how to ask without words for me to rub her belly.

Honey, I've learned, enjoys sleeping on my other side during the night. She starts out atop the covers, but by morning, she has somehow tucked herself under the floral comforter, her head atop the guest pillow like a genuine human companion.

While I stroke Cricket's belly, Honey's maw rests along my hip so I can rub the silk of her ears.

Even though the day has scarcely begun, my eyes water with emotion. I never realized I could be this happy, this content, this surrounded by love.

I kiss them both, and then vow to leave this bed.

Eventually.

Jada and I have plans to go to the fish market today. Apparently, I have been here too long not to be able to identify the different varieties of fish that are sold at the market.

I know salmon. That's the pink one. Everything else is a white fish, but apparently there is a variety called whitefish, which is its own thing, so I need to learn what the other white colored fish are.

Jada is taking it upon herself to educate me, and then we are going to swing back for the quote on the lawn for the house.

I go outside and scoop the dog poop from the backyard, whistling to myself when the birds migrate to the feeder. Aunt Em always keeps it stocked with black oil sunflower seeds. I feel like I am wrapped up in my own cartoon musical, surrounded by nature like this.

How did I live for so long without nature surrounding me and dare to call it living? Looking back, it's like I was in a waking coma surrounded by concrete and traffic. I wandered through choice after choice that was already made for me, and then felt shame when I didn't meet my parents' expectations.

Honey sniffs the grass, searching for her favorite spot, while Cricket chases a bird who taunts her by perching atop the gutter and chirping loudly.

The dew on my ankles is all the caffeine I need, but

when Jada comes to the house and insists we stop at the coffee kiosk first thing, I offer up no protest.

She holds Cricket's leash while I take Honey's. The morning sun makes the pavement glisten with pure gold. I love how seamlessly we walk together—two friends without a single care in the world.

Except, you know, figuring out who murdered Hank.

The spritely Korean woman who runs the coffee kiosk picks up a cup when she sees Jada approaching. She starts filling it up, doctoring the beverage with sugar and cream in what looks like very specific proportions.

"Have you met Bentley Cho?" Jada asks me as we make our way to her stand.

I shake my head. "I'm still meeting everybody."

By the time we reach the kiosk with an orange sign overtop the cart that reads "Ocean Potions", Bentley has a cup of coffee ready and hands it to Jada with a welcoming smile.

Jada inhales over the hot cup. "Mm. You're getting faster. It was made perfect even before I told you I was in the mood for coffee."

Bentley looks to be in her thirties, maybe six or seven years older than me. Her brimmed visor shields her kind eyes from the sun. "I put a little coconut milk in there this time. I think you'll like it."

Jada quirks an eyebrow at Bentley. "What if I was allergic to coconut?"

Bentley shrugs, the corner of her mouth lifting. "Then

I'd make you something else. But you'll like this. It's perfect. Been thinking about it all week because I was pretty sure I'd see you today."

Jada bypasses Bentley's admission that she was thinking about her all week and focuses on the coffee. I'm sure Jada is used to compliments and being adored. She's fun and pretty and has a kind word for just about everyone.

The smirk my bestie battles with tells me that the idea of Bentley thinking about her makes her happy.

Jada nudges me with her elbow. "Bentley has a gift. She can guess a person's coffee order to the T. No matter what sort of morning I've had, she makes the perfect cup to complement it. I swear, she has a very specific psychic ability." She tugs out a few dollars and rests them on the counter. "Bentley, this is Hannah Hart. She's Em's niece, new to Apple Blossom Bay."

Bentley reaches into a tin nailed to the side of her cart. She pulls out two biscuits and holds them aloft until Cricket and Honey sit nicely, salivating for the treats. "I saw the dog parade yesterday. You adopted Honey, did you?" She drops the treats and smiles while they munch happily in the sunshine.

I nod. "Sure did. Now we're one big, happy family. It's nice to meet you."

"Any friend of Jada's is, well, usually me. Good to have another Jada cheerleader around." Bentley has a welcoming smile painted with bright pink lipstick.

I chuckle at Bentley's phrasing. "That's exactly what I am. Go, Jada, go!" I pump my fist into the air while Bentley starts fixing a second cup of coffee. "Oh, I don't need…"

Jada waves off my protest. "My treat. First cup is on me. The rest of your addiction will be on you. Seriously. Don't even tell Bentley how you like it. Let her guess. I love when she gets a new person. It's like watching someone solve a complicated math problem without pen and paper. It's very cerebral."

I bite down on my lower lip, trying to keep myself from telling Bentley that full-force caffeine isn't what my body needs right now. Usually, I prefer my coffee black when I just need it for fuel to keep myself awake, which isn't all that often.

I'm used to watered down gas station beverages, so coffee has never been a huge habit for me.

Bentley must sense my creeping anxiety, because she starts to talk me through her actions while her wrists flick this way and that with the various bottles. "I'm doing half decaf, half light roast for you. I make my own simple syrups, and this one was made fresh yesterday with Ceylon cinnamon sticks and nutmeg. It's usually a fall favorite, but I have a feeling this will be the thing for you. And you're probably thinking of coconut milk, since that's what I put in Jada's. That will make it creamier and more like a treat rather than a staple."

It's hard to keep myself from intervening while I watch her work with precision, but the second she starts explaining things, my mouth begins to water. "Man, growing up here with someone who loves coffee this much had to be cool," I say to Jada.

Bentley shakes her head while she stirs. "I only moved to Apple Blossom Bay last year. I was a hedge fund manager before this. Worked for Larry in New York, actually."

My head tilts to the side. "This is quite the career change, then. Why did you make such a drastic switch?"

Bentley's smile easily breezes across her face. "My story is similar to Larry's, only mine happened a couple years after his. I came here for a conference and realized how miserable my life had been up until that point. I saw Larry here, all happy and relaxed. Figured if he could have a better life, then so could I. When the conference ended, I never went back. Quit my job and opened up Ocean Potions." She motions around her quaint kiosk. "I love it. I can work in the morning, swim in the evening, fish when-ever I get too in my head. It's the life I was working for, and I realized it didn't take retirement to get there; all it took was a cup of coffee, one really bad conference, and Larry proving to me that a better quality of life is possible."

Bentley hands me my cup and waits for me to inhale.

The aroma is like nothing I realized could exist in a cup of coffee. The cinnamon isn't a normal muted flavor, but an experience I feel down to my toes. "Oh, wow. This smells incredible. I want to live directly above this scent all day."

Bentley beams at the compliment. "That's the idea. You'll never go back to a boring cup ever again." She motions around her. "And now that you're in Apple Blossom Bay, you'll never go back to life before you moved here."

I inhale happily, agreeing wholeheartedly with Bentley. I cannot imagine living anywhere else than this sweet ocean town.

21

COFFEE AND FISH

I mull over Bentley's life story while she and Jada pet the dogs in front of the Ocean Potions coffee kiosk. Bentley does a good covert flirt, which is too subtle for Jada to pick up on.

I decide to be brave and engage in conversation with the new person. "I did that, too," I tell Bentley when she mentions how much she loves living here. "Not the starting up a coffee cart part, but the leaving normal life behind to live here. I wasn't sure how long I was going to be here, but now I can't see myself going back. I can breathe." As if on cue, the breeze picks up and sends a fresh dose of the ocean my way. "I didn't realize I'd not been exhaling before I moved here."

Bentley stands, her straight black hair whooshing away from her face with the breeze. "Funny how you can get by in life for years without breathing. Then once you get a whiff of true happiness, you realize you've been suffocating all along." She extends her hand to me. "Welcome to Apple Blossom Bay, Hannah. It's a good place for an outsider to make themselves a solid home. I hope you find your coffee cart, whatever it may be."

The corner of my mouth crooks. I love working at the grocery store. But whenever I get home and want a little "me" time, I am either baking dog biscuits, reading my prairie novels, or putting together puzzles.

Or robbing City Hall.

It's a very small path of interests I hold, but the moment I think about making a new dog biscuit flavor, the image of a cinnamon cookie comes to mind. Perhaps it could have a cinnamon cream drizzle over the top.

I hold my cup aloft. "Bentley, tell me about this cinnamon syrup. You made it?"

"Sure did. It's Ceylon cinnamon."

My nose scrunches. "What's the difference between that and regular cinnamon?"

Bentley crosses her arms and leans her hip on the side of the kiosk, gearing up to educate me. "Ceylon cinnamon is better for your liver than the regular ground stuff you find at the grocery store (which is usually cassia cinnamon). It's also a bit sweeter, so you don't have to use as much in the syrups to really make the flavor shine."

I absorb the new information, making a mental note to get Ceylon cinnamon the next time I go grocery shopping. My dogs deserve the best of the best in their treats.

I can picture myself baking for hours endless varieties of dog biscuits for no reason other than the fun of it.

It's silly, really, wanting to bake dog biscuits for a living. Surely that's not a job. If someone bakes dog biscuits for profit, they probably also sell pet care things, which I have no interest in doing.

A dog bakery?

I inhale the coffee, my shoulders relaxing when the cinnamon notes flood my nose, pushing the problem of logic far from my mind.

What a beautiful life that would be—baking dog treats all the livelong day and handing them out to the pups who pass by. I'm sure there are more exciting professions, and more lucrative, for sure. But when I picture myself wearing some sort of decorative dog-themed apron, my hair up in a messy bun and peanut butter treats scattered across the counter, a smile spreads through my soul.

It's okay to daydream. Though, even imagining a life like that makes me worry I might be looked down on for considering something of which my parents would not approve.

Bentley jerks her chin at Jada by way of a parting gesture, and then does the same to me. She tugs down the brim of her visor, tipping it in our direction. "See you tomorrow, ladies."

"Tomorrow? Is there an event in town?" I ask Jada as we walk away with our dogs.

"No, she's just very sure of herself. Bentley knows we'll

drink our coffees and be back to order more tomorrow. I swear it's my Saturday tradition, but it's turning into a Saturday and Sunday addiction."

I chuckle while I inhale the fragrant beverage. "If it tastes as good as it smells, I'll be back tomorrow, for sure."

Jada grins at me. "It's decided, then. Every Saturday and Sunday morning, we start our days at the coffee cart, Hannah Hart." She snickers at her rhyme.

I hold back the tease I am sure Jada doesn't want to hear. I know Bentley will surely be glad to see Jada twice on the weekend. I could see the smile aimed at her, and the twinkle in Bentley's eyes whenever Jada looks her way.

But Jada seems not to want to comment on Bentley's silent affection for her, or perhaps she hasn't noticed it, so I keep my mouth shut about the whole thing.

I have plans with my new bestie, and I couldn't be happier.

We walk together toward the fish market, where I am surprised I am able to recognize several people. I wave to Mrs. Finch before I remember what a sourpuss she is, and that she probably doesn't like being greeted so gregariously.

Still, I go all in while we walk in her direction toward the first booth in the market. "Good morning, Mrs. Finch. Nice day out, isn't it?"

Mrs. Finch narrows one eye at me as if I've asked her if she likes to eat lizards. "What of it?"

I turn to the booth she's at, determined not to let her

contaminate my good mood. "What kind of fish is this?" I ask Jada.

Before Jada can answer, Mrs. Finch scoffs. "That's a trout. Everyone knows that."

Jada's hand goes to her hip as she squares her shoulders to the older woman. "You're charming as usual, Mrs. Finch. Any particular bee crawl into your bonnet today?"

Mrs. Finch's upper lip curls in Honey's direction. "I'm glad that mutt isn't peeing on my petunias anymore. But honestly, the damage is done. They'll never grow as they should. I'll be repairing that soil for years."

Honey whimpers, inching away from the older woman's glower.

I frown at the surly neighbor. I want to shield Honey with my body. "Well, you could always call up that lawn-care service who asked if you needed help with anything. Maybe they can fix the flowers for you."

Mrs. Finch points a crooked finger at me. "That kid doesn't know how to rub two sticks together. Do you think I'd trust him with my petunias? He had that look about him."

I tilt my head to the side. "What look?"

The corners of her mouth crinkle as her lips purse. "The kind of look that says he's up to no good."

Jada rolls her eyes. "Good to see you, Mrs. Finch. You are a ray of sunshine, as usual." Jada bumps her hip to mine and guides me to the next booth. "Don't pay her any mind. She's always like that."

"Yikes. What could the lawncare guy possibly have done or said to make her think he was incompetent?"

"He was upright and made direct eye contact, I'm guessing. That's about all it takes for her to form an unpleasant opinion about a person." Jada motions to the next booth. "But that's not what we're here for. We want to look at the fish, so here we are. That was trout over there, but this booth is mostly catfish. Everyone sells a little bit of everything, but they each have a specialty, so they don't crowd each other out of the business." She pounds the fist of the vendor in greeting. The woman looks to be in her forties, her brimmed hat shielding her freckled face from the sun. "This is Sharon. She is an artist when it comes to catfish. I mean, no matter how you want it cut, there's not a way she can't do it."

Sharon fans her face at the compliment. "That's what I need to call my booth: The Catfish Artist."

That's a far sight better than her sign that simply advertises "Catfish".

Randy—the man who sells lobsters on the strip—waves at the two of us. "Morning, kids! You didn't bring me a coffee? The nerve!"

Jada chuckles as she guzzles a gluttonous gulp just to make Randy laugh.

It is easy to see why Jada is beloved in this town. She is friendly and has a kind thing to say about nearly everyone we encounter. I love strolling by her side, feeling like I'm part of the cool crowd because she is introducing me to everyone.

One by one, I learn the names and kinds of fish the various vendors sell, but it's difficult to commit the fish to memory, since they all look similar. While I don't know much about any of it, as my palate never progressed beyond canned tuna, now that I am a resident of Apple Blossom Bay, I decide to put my mind to use, learning all about the fish here, and the welcoming people who catch and sell them.

With Jada by my side, I am fairly certain that Apple Blossom Bay will feel like the home I never had in no time.

22

WALL-TO-WALL LAWNCARE

*A*fter Mrs. Finch's dressing down of the lawncare guy when he came soliciting around her neighborhood, I am determined to be extra kind to him when he shows up at Aunt Em's.

My aunt is on a call, trying to find the right house to sell to a couple who wants to move here, so when the doorbell rings, it's me who answers the door, along with both my dogs.

Cricket does her job of alerting me to the fact that the doorbell rang, and Honey sticks by my side, unwilling to ever be more than two feet away from me in any given moment.

When I open the door, a rust-haired guy in his early twenties greets me, yellow uniform shirt untucked and stained. He sniffles, wipes his nose, and then extends the dirty hand to me.

I try not to grimace at the offering. "Good morning. Wall-to-Wall Lawncare?"

The guy nods, showing me the logo on his yellow shirt. "Yep. You wanted a quote?"

I move a foot forward to step outside with him, but I freeze when Honey growls.

The sound is so unusual that I don't know what to do at first. Honey's not exactly the friendly sort when it comes to interacting with others, but I've never heard her growl at anyone before.

"Sorry, give me a second." I bend down to run my fingers over Honey's short fur. "What's wrong, babe?"

Honey sticks close to me, as if trying to communicate some dire need. Her eyes are larger than usual, telling me something is very wrong, indeed.

"You want to go outside?"

Honey whines but doesn't make a move toward the backdoor.

When Honey makes it clear that she will not tolerate me being more than an inch from her side, I glance up apologetically to the guy. "Sorry, she's never like this. Can you give the yard a look without me? I'd like the lawn cut once a week, if possible, and the hedges trimmed so my aunt doesn't have to worry about them. How much would that be?"

The guy glances warily at Honey instead of looking at me when he replies. "I'll give the lawn a look and come back with a price. Do you want the flowerbeds weeded or the gutters blown out?"

"Yes to the gutters, but my aunt likes fussing with the flowerbeds, so she probably would like to do those herself." Honey barks, which also is unlike her. "Honey, honestly. What's going on?" I shut the door so I can focus on the issue I don't understand.

The guy goes out into the yard, wandering around the house with his clipboard. I feel awful that my dog is unhappy with the man, but there's nothing more I can do than apologize and keep Honey in the house.

My hand runs over Honey while a low growl peppers her breathing. I can tell she wants me to know she is unhappy. Maybe she is unused to having a man in this house, and she's letting me hear her unhappiness. Perhaps he smells like something she doesn't like.

Whatever it is, I opt to keep her inside, in case she gets the urge to bite the stranger.

"It's okay, baby. Honestly, I don't know how to tell you that sometimes people come to the front door who don't have treats for you on hand."

Cricket takes a note from Honey, acting as the corgi's sentry when the guy comes back to the front door a few minutes later. Cricket barks, though the sound isn't all that intimidating.

"Sorry," I say again as I stand. I open the door but make sure the dogs know they are not to come out with me. "Stay, you two troublemakers." I tsk them with an exasper-ated smile. "I swear, I don't know what's gotten into them. I think it's that they expect every time they see a stranger, that person's going to have treats for them at the ready."

The guy swipes the back of his hand under his runny nose. Then he takes his pen and jots something down on his clipboard. "I've got the price here for your lawn. The hedges are extra, and I can do those twice a year."

I nod, as if I have any semblance of a clue for how to accurately judge if I am being charged a fair price. "That's fine. And the spring cleanup?"

He points to the gutters above us. "These are pretty clogged. That's the thing about not doing a fall cleanup. They need extra oomph in the spring." He jots down another price.

By the time it's all added up, my eyes bug at the number. "Wow. I didn't realize it would be that much. Can I take a week and think about it? I only just started working, stocking shelves at the grocery store in town. I might need to wait for the paychecks to start coming in."

The guy tilts his head to the side, sizing me up anew. "Over at the Forgotten Stock Market? You work for Larry?"

I nod, smiling that we know the same people. "Sure do."

The man's face sours. "You have my old job. I was working there, stocking shelves up until last month." His upper lip curls. "It was the worst. You have my sympathies."

I grimace. "Actually, the job suits me well. But I can see how it wouldn't appeal to everyone."

He lets out a "pfft" sound. "That's an understatement. Though, maybe it wasn't the job itself. That was fine. Mindless, but fine. It was the pay. Larry is such a tightfisted weasel." He leans in conspiratorially. "He won big in his poker game recently, you know. How's that for karma taking a nap? Two years stocking shelves there with no raise. That's not how you treat your loyal employees. Such a waste of my life."

I don't know what to say to that, so I go for empathy. "Sounds like it was a rough time for you. I'm sorry to hear that."

"That's putting it mildly. Make sure to always ask for what you're worth. When you don't get it, be prepared to walk. This job is far better." He motions to the logo on his yellow shirt. "I get plenty of fresh air, and I don't have Larry on my case, telling me I'm falling behind and I need to stay on top of the stock." He rolls his eyes. "I mean, give me a break. It's stocking shelves, not rocket science. It's not like if we don't have all seven varieties of peanut butter on display, the town will starve."

I don't comment on his demeaning remarks of the importance of keeping a store well stocked. Instead, I take the piece of paper he hands me, reading his name scribbled at the bottom.

"Thanks, Wally. I'm glad you found a job that suits you. It can be miserable if you're in the wrong profession."

"Hear, hear. How did you learn about the company? It's for my boss."

"I took a slip of paper from the flyer at the grocery store. You also gave Mrs. Finch and Hank a quote. I figure if people have seen you around town, that's good. Nice to hire local and all that."

Wally's face twists. "I never gave Hank a quote."

My mouth screws to the side. "Oh? Mrs. Finch said she saw you go in to talk with Hank after trying to bid her house." My pointer finger rests on my chin. "Though, maybe you were just hanging out with him. Everyone here is so friendly. I love it. Or maybe it was a coworker of yours."

Wally gives a noncommittal grunt before reminding me to call him for the lawn work soon before the company gets too busy to schedule new clients for the season. He tucks his clipboard under his arm and returns to his truck.

After Wally drives off, I have an unsettled feeling in my stomach. While I want to hire someone to do the work for my aunt because it would be a nice gift for her, I'm not sure I can afford that if I'm going to be feeding Honey the pricier stuff to which she's grown accustomed.

I really can't compromise on Honey's creature comforts —not after all she's been through.

I tuck the paper into my back pocket as I turn to my dogs upon reentering the house. They have not stopped making their presence known, even through the closed door.

While I cannot afford to hire Wally just yet, I know I

can sacrifice the rest of my weekend and roll up my sleeves myself to get this yard into shape.

I tug out my phone and call the one person I wouldn't mind sweating beside. "Hey, Jada. How do you feel about yardwork? I'll pay you in Sunday's coffee bill. Jumbo sized."

23

HELP WITH THE GUTTERS

I sweat through my t-shirt already, and there is no end in sight. "Jada, are you staying hydrated?"

"Does coffee count? Because if it does, then yes."

I snicker while I clip at the hedge with the giant scissors I found in Aunt Em's garage. "I'm thinking that does the opposite of hydrate a person. Drink water, or you'll lose steam halfway through the job."

Are huge scissors the size of my femur easy to maneuver with one hand? No.

Does that make me rise to the challenge? Absolutely yes.

Will I have a bruise on my right forearm? One hundred percent.

One of the many reasons I like Jada is because she doesn't treat me as if I can't do something just because she can't picture how the task might work if a person is sans a right hand. She watches surreptitiously as I use my forearm in ways most people wouldn't fathom.

Jada stands from the flower bed with a groan. "We're not already halfway through? Is there some sort of time warp that slows everything down when you have to do manual labor?"

I chuckle at her exasperation because it is not much different from my own. "We've mown the front yard and the back. You're weeding the flower beds and I'm nearly done with the bottom half of these hedges. There can't be much more work, can there?"

Jada hangs her head. "Get out the paper. That quote sheet Wally gave you."

I uncrinkle the piece of paper, which we have been using as a checklist of all the things we are going to get done before we call it a day. "Ah, jeez. We've still got the gutters, the mulch, and the top halves of these hedges, which I don't know how to do because we don't have a ladder."

Jada takes out her phone. "Where are the reinforcements I ordered? Come on, now."

"Reinforcements?" I ask, stretching out my back while I give my arms a break from the loppers. I can already feel the blisters forming on my palm and a burgeoning bruise on my forearm.

Jada nods, and then points to the driveway. "Finally!"

She lets loose a sigh of exasperation. "Brothers, am I right?"

"Huh?" I turn my head, my eyes widening when Jada's brother gets out of his pickup truck. My pitch shoots up an octave. "You asked Niles to come over?"

Jada shakes out her hands. "Of course. Did you really think we were going to do this all ourselves? This takes a team, for sure. Besides, like you said, we need a ladder."

My neck shrinks as insecurity washes over me. "You should have told me you invited him!" I whisper-shout, panic pinching my tone.

Jada quirks an eyebrow at me. "Why?" When I straighten out my sweat-stained t-shirt and redo my messy ponytail, Jada's eyes widen through a knowing chuckle. "Interesting. I'll admit, I didn't see that coming."

"See what coming?" I ask her, not wanting the answer. It shouldn't matter that her brother is the prettiest person on the planet, or that I am a sweaty slob the one time he comes over. I have absolutely no chance with a man like Niles, who is put together and perfect.

"You're blushing!" Jada whispers, scandalized and overjoyed.

"I am not! I'm sweating, is all."

Niles opens the tailgate of his truck and hefts out a ladder. "I hear you two need help. Pesky little sister, volunteering me for work on my day off. Sounds about right."

Jada motions to the house. "Hey, how many times has Em baked you cookies? How many times has she made you chicken noodle soup when you were too sick to go to the store to buy a can of it for yourself?"

He has a lighthearted bop in his step as he makes his way to us. "Only Em can get this kind of work out of me on a Saturday."

Niles props the aluminum ladder to the front of the house. "I take it I'm on gutter duty?"

Jada gives him a hearty thumbs up. "Anything with a ladder is all you." The second Niles turns his back to her, Jada fixes me with an evil grin. "Hannah, could you hold the ladder still for Niles? Can't have him falling on the job."

I shoot a panicked look at her. "Uh, sure." But I want to tell her that I should be far, far away from Niles, lest I say something stupid or blush in plain sight.

Niles puts on work gloves and climbs up the ladder, grimacing at what awaits him. "Remind me to do her gutters in the fall, so there isn't this much buildup."

Even his grimace is gorgeous. This is going to be a problem.

I stand at the base of the ladder, holding it still and squinting up at him. "I really appreciate this. I was going to hire someone, but the costs kept adding up. Plus, Honey didn't like the guy, so I didn't want him at the house if it was going to pupset her."

Niles chuckles at my verbal slip. "Pupset? No, we don't want Honey pupset."

I shrink at how idiotic I sound. "Upset. You know what I mean."

Honey pants at my side, not giving Niles the same ruffled treatment she gave Wally. She doesn't seem to mind Niles' presence on the property at all.

I guess it wasn't that it was a man coming to our home that set her off.

Maybe it was the fact that Wally constantly wipes his nose and then touches things he means to hand to you.

Maybe Niles has a charm to him that even extends to dogs.

Whatever it is, Honey has made it clear by the wagging of her tail that Niles is welcome, while Wally is not.

Niles keeps his eyes on the gutters while he talks to me. "I love Emily. Like my annoying little sister said, Em takes care of us all the time without thinking twice. I didn't realize she needed help with her gutters and whatnot. Any time she needs help, let me know, okay?"

Jada calls over to us. "That would be easier for her to do if you gave Hannah your phone number."

I make to protest the blatant pushing together Jada is trying to do, but Niles thinks nothing of it.

Obviously, because I am not in his league.

"That's a good idea." Niles waits for me to pull out my phone before he calls down the string of digits to me.

"Thanks," I say, then pocket my phone so I can hold onto the ladder. "I really do appreciate the help. I was hoping Jada and I could get it done today without bothering anyone else, but it's more work than I realized. Plus, I don't have a ladder, which seems to be the main tool in cleaning out gutters and doing the tops of the hedges."

"Like I said, it's not a problem. Em's the best."

Once Niles starts tossing gutter debris down onto the freshly mown lawn, I give him a wide berth, so I don't get soggy leaves tangled in my hair.

"Honey didn't like Wally?" Niles asks, starting up a conversation from atop the ladder.

"Started growling the second he came by. It's not like her, but I guess we're still getting used to each other. I'm learning her cues."

Niles keeps his eyes on his task. "I've never seen Honey growl at anybody. She's too scared of her own shadow to make an angry noise." He shrugs as he digs into the gutter with his gloved fist. "The fact that she growled at someone? Either she's much more relaxed and vocal, now that she's got you and Cricket, or she really didn't like Wally." He shrugs. "That's not an unpopular opinion."

"Oh, yeah? Wally isn't your pavorite ferson in Apple Blossom Bay?"

Niles chuckles. "No. Wally's not my 'pavorite ferson' or my favorite person. When he worked at the grocery store, nothing was where it was supposed to be. It was all half-stocked, and when you would ask him if they had something in the back, he would be gone for like, twenty minutes. Then he'd come back and have no idea what he'd been sent back there to look for."

Jada chimes in. "We didn't realize it could be any other way until you started working there. Now the store looks perfect. It's clean. Everything is where it should be. The shelves are stocked. I swear, once word starts circulating that the grocery store is top notch, I'll bet business will be booming for Larry. There were many times I just changed what I planned on making for the week because I knew I wouldn't be able to find it at the store."

My hand goes over my heart. "I don't care if you two are making all of that up to make me feel valued, or if it's actually true. Thank you for saying that. I love it when things are in order." I motion around to the yard. "That's what I want for Aunt Em. I want this to be a place she can relax. I want her to be able to play and enjoy, rather than spend all her time doing upkeep. She's been so good to me."

Niles stops to peer down at my red and sweaty face. "You're really good to her. I like that. Emily is awesome. She's amazing to everybody. Always helping, always doing, always spreading the love. The fact that she's got you around, thinking about how to get the weeds out of her life so she can play more? The whole town benefits when Em can play more. She's the type to spread the joy far and wide. The more she has, the more she gives."

I smile up at him, soaking in the rays of his compliments to my aunt that keep on coming. "That's sweet of you to say. I really like living here, and she's the best part of it for me."

Niles tears his gaze from my face and then turns his

chin to the gutters. "We like having you here, Hannah Hart."

Jada waits to make sure her brother isn't looking and then does a giddy dance, complete with miming clapping her hands that my brother said something nice to me.

Because he's a nice person, not because someone of his caliber would ever think I'm on his level.

I really like the way he says my whole name.

Once Niles finishes the gutters on this side of the house, he takes a break to drink some water.

I go back to trimming the lower half of the hedges that I can reach. I tuck his kind words away while I clip the errant branches, so the row is neat. I want it to look like a wall, perfectly in order, as if nature has done its best to comply with my aesthetic of happiness.

I really hope Aunt Em likes this.

The three of us work in companionable silence as Jada turns on the best of Dolly Parton to keep us moving at a decent clip. She has the confidence to sing along at whatever volume she feels like, while I keep my humming muted because I occasionally go off-key, and I don't want Niles to know that.

Dolly would be ashamed that I make myself smaller and quieter because I opt for shyness rather than living my off-key truth out loud.

But Dolly is awesome, so I'm guessing she would hug me either way.

I love the fresh air, the sunshine beating down on my

skin, the Vitamin D soaking into my pores while I spend my Saturday taking care of my aunt with two genuinely good people and my sweet dogs.

I whistle to the tune until Jada breaks the rhythm. "Uh, Hannah? You don't happen to collect kitchen knives and then leave them laying around, do you?"

I frown at her odd question. "Huh?"

Jada stands with a long knife in her hand that would normally be used to cut giant hunks of meat, not trim weeds. "Did you lose this? I found it in the flower bed."

My mouth drops open at the sight of the dirty knife out in the open like that. "That's not Em's, and I didn't bring any knives with me to Apple Blossom Bay. Aunt Em's knives all have purple handles."

Jada nods. "That's right. So, this one isn't yours?"

I shake my head.

Niles finishes the last bit of the gutters on the row, and then walks himself slowly down the rungs. He studies the knife with unhappiness clouding his features. "That's been sitting in the flower beds? I'm surprised Cricket or Honey didn't find it. It's good you did, Jada. The little babies might've hurt themselves." He reaches down and lifts up Cricket, holding her on his hip as if she's his toddler.

Cricket is not shy, and kisses his cheek happily.

If I wasn't attracted to Niles before, I am hopelessly smitten now.

I purse my lips and turn back to the matter at hand. "That knife can't have been here long. I mean, the dogs are always in the yard. Surely they would have come across the knife already. And Aunt Em was just in the backyard earlier this week. She would have found it."

Honey barks, letting me know she is unhappy with the knife being in Jada's hand.

Jada's lips purse as Honey moves toward the dirty knife. My corgi's barks sound like an alert to which we all must pay attention. Jada's gaze meets mine, identical wariness shining through. "I don't think this landed here by mistake," Jada announces, taking a step back. "And I don't think this has been here long, since Honey's having a reaction to it."

I didn't expect a police car to come to my house on this sunshining Saturday, but when a quick call to Aunt Em confirms that she didn't use or notice a knife in the flowerbed, I know our weekend is about to take an unfortunate turn.

When Deputy Hanson steps out of his squad car with his partner by his side, my stomach drops. Even though we made the call to invite them over to take the knife and give the backyard a once over, my nerves are on edge.

"That's not just any knife," I say to Jada, voicing the conclusion I can tell we have both reached at the same time.

Jada holds the weapon out from her body as if it is a snake, wincing at Honey's bark. "This has to be the knife that killed Hank. Honey wouldn't be this upset about a regular kitchen knife."

Niles flags down the officers, waving them toward us. "I think we found a murder weapon."

But the deputy doesn't look relieved. He moves onto my lawn with a grave expression weighting his tired features. "Hannah Hart? I'm going to need you to come with me to the station."

My mouth drops open. "Me? What for?"

Deputy Hanson points to the knife displayed in plain view. "Because we got word that the murder weapon was found on your property." He lowers his chin at me. "Not much of a point in denying it. Come with us, young lady."

Jada gapes at the deputy. "But we're the ones who called it in! That's how you found out about the murder weapon in the first place."

Terror rips through my veins. I back up, my fight or flight instinct kicking into high gear. If I was sweating before, I am positively dehydrating now.

"There's more to this investigation than your phone call. Someone else called it in, too. We'll discuss it at the station."

Jada hands over the knife and trots to my side. "I'll go with you. All they need to do is cross you off their list of suspects. That's easy because you're innocent."

Niles stands on my other side. The siblings hem me in to keep my knees from going out from under me.

While I nod and comply, the deputy looks at me as if I am the prime suspect in Hank's murder investigation.

24

MY HORRIBLE CRIMES

y stomach is in knots, and not just because I am being investigated for the murder of the man whose dog I now own. Beside me is my aunt, who doesn't look the least bit concerned that her niece is being questioned in a murder investigation, or that she has been called in because the knife was found on her property.

Oh, to have her confidence.

She runs her purple painted nails over my back to soothe me, the sleeve of her fluttery floral blouse trickling over my arm. "Now, now. It's nothing. So the knife was found in my yard. That's not exactly a smoking gun."

I hold my face in my hand. "It's worse than that! It's a bloody knife! Aunt Em, I swear, I don't know how it got in the backyard!"

Of all things, my aunt chuckles. "I know that, Hannah

Grapefruit. There's not a doubt in my mind that we've been set up."

I turn my head slowly toward her, taking in her relaxed expression. "What? You think the knife was planted there?" I ignore my phone when it rings.

"Of course." Em indulges in a long sigh. "The question is, who would want to frame us? And is it me they mean to have framed, or you? Or were we just a convenient stop along the way? It can't have been at the house long; the dogs would have found it."

Jada holds my hand. She hasn't left my side this entire time. Though I am in need of a shower and am emotionally distraught, she is not put off by the messy nature of my day. "It's going to be just fine. It wasn't you who killed Hank and hid the murder weapon in the flowerbed, so there's nothing to worry about."

Aunt Em is the picture of poise. She is wearing a long, flowing skirt in her favorite color. Her black hair is tied up in a crocheted headband. She looks like she is ready for a fashionable stroll along the beach, rather than an interrogation.

I, on the other hand, look like I have been doing yardwork all morning. I am sweating my anxiety out through my tear ducts and pores. My face is red, and my nerves are at critical mass.

When Deputy Hanson comes out and motions for me to go into his backroom, I lose all feeling in my hand. I only know I am moving because Jada takes me with her, going into the hot seat with me because she is that good of a friend.

When the door shuts behind us, I burst into tears. Suddenly, every horrible thing I have ever done comes vomiting out of me in a manic rant. "I sometimes put egg cartons into the trash instead of the recycling! When I'm tired, sometimes I hit the snooze button twice, which is rude to anyone else in the house. There are days that I see crumbs on the counter, but I don't wipe them off! When I was driving here from Chicago, I went five miles over the speed limit the entire time for no reason." On my left hand, I touch my thumb to each of my fingers while I fret aloud. "I didn't study for my finals the last year of college. I didn't even care if I passed or failed. What kind of a sick person does that?"

Jada's hand goes over her mouth.

I can feel it. Jada is learning the worst parts of me, and she is pulling back. I am losing my favorite non-family person in the world because I am an awful human being. I will confess every bad thing I've ever done to the deputy, so he knows I am a horrible person, but not a murderer.

I should shut up, but more spews out of me. "This one time, I told my professor I didn't have time to complete my essay, but that wasn't true. I lied to his face! I just didn't want to do the essay. Instead of doing the assignment, I watched six straight hours of past Westminster Dog Shows. I lied! And the worst part was he gave me extra time to complete the essay. I'm the worst person in the world!" I fan my face, wishing I could just keep quiet. "And the sound system! I did it!"

I bury my face in my hand, disgusted that so many sins are coming to light.

I wait, standing near the door, bracing myself for the handcuffs.

Instead, the only sound I hear is... Is that laughter?

Jada's hand drops from her mouth. A bubbly, giddy sound spills through the interrogation room. "Wow. I mean, just wow. Thank goodness you confessed to all those crimes. I'm not sure I want to be seen with you now."

Horror washes through me. "I deserve that. I'm so sorry! I didn't kill Hank, but I did all those other things."

Jada shakes her head, her arms going around me as if I am a basket case in need of solid footing. "I was kidding! You're not a bad person, Hannah. You, me, Deputy Hanson and the entire town knows it wasn't you."

I motion to my form as self-inflicted guilt for all the wrongs I have done wafts off me. "But I'm the perfect suspect! I'm new in town. I adopted Hank's dog—there's my motivation. The knife was found in my backyard. I'm clearly guilty, even though I didn't do it!"

Jada holds me tight, shushing me not to shut me up, but to calm my spiking nerves. "Hey, I believe you. I'm the one who found the knife. Maybe I planted it there to frame you."

I sniffle on her shoulder. "But you didn't do that! You

found something because you were helping me out on your day off. You had nothing to do with any of it."

"I know," she tells me in a soothing manner. "Just like you." Her hand smooths over my back. "So, if it wasn't me and it wasn't you, then who could it have been? Who else was at the house between the last time Em weeded the flower beds and this morning?"

My chin rests on her shoulder, finding enough solace to gather my thoughts. "I don't know. Phyllis, Edna, and Dorothy came over, but that's not unusual."

"Good. Who else?"

I squeeze Jada tighter. "I don't want to point the finger at Phyllis, Edna, or Dorothy! They clearly didn't do anything wrong."

"I know, and that's not what you're doing. But we're brainstorming. Who else was in the yard?"

I bury my face in Jada's shoulder, grateful for the safety she offers me. I hold onto her, wracking my brain until a face comes into view. "I mean, Wally was there giving me a quote, but I called him to come over. He didn't nefariously show up for no reason. I asked him to size up the property to give me a quote for the yardwork." I gasp, my fingers bunching in Jada's shirt. "I framed him! I didn't mean to, but that's what I did!"

Jada's chest vibrates, and I can tell she is holding back laughter. "You did nothing of the sort. You didn't have the knife that killed Hank, so you didn't frame Wally. You're not even calling him guilty. You're just giving old Deputy

Hanson here information so he can sniff out the right suspect."

The deputy clears his throat, letting us know he has been ignored long enough, and does not appreciate being called old. "The knife you two found matches the stab wounds on Hank, as far as I can tell, so I think we've got the murder weapon. I'm not convinced it was you who killed Hank, Hannah, but all that other stuff you've done?" He tsks me, shaking his head. "I'm going to write you up for not recycling that egg carton."

I turn to him, my chin downward in complete submission, accepting that I should absolutely pay for this crime of being careless. "Yes, sir. I deserve that." I hold out my arms, awaiting the slap of the cuffs.

Deputy Hanson chuckles at my sincerity, his slightly pooched belly jiggling in time with the sound. "I'm joking, you know. We don't actually write people up for using their garbage bins on recyclables." He tilts his head to the side, sizing up my obvious distress. "Wow. I can't imagine what you would be like if you actually did try to commit a crime."

"You know I didn't do it?" I ask him, blinking at his ruddy features to make sure I am hearing him correctly.

He chortles at my confusion. "Either that, or you're a stellar actress."

I shake my head so fast, Jada giggles at me. "I didn't have anything to do with Hank's murder! I don't know how that knife got into the yard, and neither does Aunt Em."

The deputy holds up his hands. "I believe you. I'll talk to your aunt to see when the last time was that she was in the backyard in that particular area, so we can narrow down the list of suspects. Wally, Dorothy, Edna, and Phyllis? Anyone else?"

I cradle my head in my hand. "I'm not calling them guilty, you realize. I'm just telling you who was in the backyard."

The deputy holds up a hand to stave off my discomfort. "I understand that."

After a few more back and forths, and the promise that I will always recycle the cardboard egg cartons, Jada escorts me out of the backroom and into the sun, where I can finally breathe, now that the finger isn't being pointed at me or my aunt.

But still the question haunts me. Who could possibly have put the knife in our backyard?

CRICKET AND HONEY

When Jada and I get home after a stop at an ice cream shop for what Jada calls "necessary therapy" once Em and I are declared free to go, I am shocked to find the gutters done around the entire house, and the tops of the hedges trimmed in a lovely, flat line across the top where I could not reach with the loppers. Not only that, but there is no yard waste to bag up and deal with.

I gape at the beautiful yard. "Did... Did your brother finish the job on his own?"

Jada examines the landscape appreciatively. "Looks to be that way. Aw, that's nice. Now we can relax."

Tenderness touches my heart. "I can't believe Niles did that. He didn't have to keep going with everything after we left. That's real nice of him."

If only he had a selfish, mean personality, then I could get over my crush quicker.

Jada shrugs as she moves to the backyard to survey the scene. "He has his moments." She pulls out her phone, I'm guessing to text a thank you to Niles.

"Tell him I appreciate this," I request, looking around at the backyard in all its glory. "This is what I wanted—for Aunt Em to have the bigger things taken care of so she didn't have to get on a ladder or hire someone to do the gutters. She's done so much for me, taking me in like this. I wanted to repay the kindness."

Jada glances up after putting her phone in her pocket. "Well, it's gorgeous back here. I..." But her chipper demeanor fades when her gaze fixes on a point in the corner of the yard. "What is that?"

Jada beelines to the birdbath, her jaw tight and her gait stiff.

My heart sinks when I see the scope of the problem. "It's a man's baseball cap. Looks old and faded." I glance to the hedges, wondering just how strong the wind would have to be to blow the thing clear across the yard from the hedges Niles was working on to the back corner of the yard. "It can't belong to the neighbor. It must belong to Niles." I frown at my own suggestion. "Though, he wasn't wearing a baseball cap when he got here. Maybe he put it on after we left."

Jada shakes her head over and over before words come to her. "My brother doesn't have a hat like that. It would cover the fade he loves to show off. But I'll give you one guess as to who did have a hat like that."

I tilt my head to the side as different faces flash through my mind. My stomach sinks when a grim guess comes to me. "Was it Hank's hat?"

Jada nods unhappily. "He wore the same faded green trucker hat every day. Fishing, shopping, walking around. I'm sure he even wore the thing to church and fancy events." She pinches the bridge of her nose. "This is not good."

I tug my phone out of my pocket and put in a call to the deputy, whom I am guessing won't be all that pleased to hear from me twice in one day. I see that I have missed two calls from the same number I don't recognize, but I don't have the interest or time to listen to the voicemail the caller left. I need a police officer here to deal with Hank's hat.

Jada makes a point of not touching the hat, backing up while I tell the deputy what we found.

Of all the phone numbers I have programmed, the fact that the deputy is in my phone is not lost on me. I never had this much use for law enforcement before I moved here.

"No, it definitely wasn't there when we left to come talk to you earlier," I tell Deputy Hanson. "Yep, I'll be here. We won't touch it. Come on over whenever you can."

My shoulders slump as Jada takes her time looking around the yard for anything else that might have been planted here while we were out. It is becoming clearer and clearer that either I am being framed, or Aunt Em is being set up to take the fall for the guilty person's crime.

"Why?" I ask Jada when she comes back to my side. "Why would anyone want to frame Aunt Em?"

Jada quirks an eyebrow at me. "Um, I think the real question is who is trying to frame you?"

My face pulls at the question. "I'm new here. I couldn't possibly have any enemies. Not that Aunt Em would have any either." I open the backdoor, which we always leave unlocked.

Cricket's footsteps come skittering toward me, her tail wagging as if nothing nefarious has happened today at all. She licks my hand when I reach down to pet her. Then she barks, as if she means to tell me something important. She jumps on her hind legs, her front paws landing on my knee.

I'll have to train her not to do that.

Later.

"Yes, baby. I love you, too."

I go with Jada to the kitchen table, where we sit to rest. What feels like the weight of the world has come to rest on our shoulders.

Jada leans her elbows on the table while she massages her temples. "This day is so weird. I feel like we need to take a nap to start fresh. If only that would undo everything."

I fiddle with the hem of my shirt, mulling over the start

of all of this. "I didn't know Hank. I'm not sure I ever met him, even in passing. Now I have his dog, and I'm the one who saw him how he was when the killer left him so cruelly in the backroom of the grocery store." I shake my head. "Who would do that?"

Jada closes her eyes. "There's no logic we could ever connect with when it's a killer involved. I feel awful for Hank."

"I know nothing about him, other than that he fished, had a nice boat, and loved his dog."

Jada sits back in her seat. "What do you want to know?"

I shrug. "Anything that pushes out the image of him lying there, dead."

Jada crosses her arms over her chest. "He called me 'Jada-Joy'. I never particularly cared for the nickname, but now I wish he would call out to me in the fish market one more time. 'Hey, Jada-Joy. Are you still the best kinder-garten teacher in the world?' Stuff like that. Always had something nice to say, even if it was a silly dad joke. He was a good guy. Good person." She smiles softly to herself. "This one time, I saw him with his mini cooler and Honey on the dock, getting his boat ready to go out for the morn-ing. I waved to him and asked him if he was excited to catch a fish for the day. He said he wasn't going fishing; he was going to sit on the water to clear his head." Jada goes silent for a few beats. I can tell she is picturing Hank's visage. "I like the people who get it. I live on the water, so I understand the need to stare at the waves and let them untangle your thoughts. People who do that are like me. I feel a connection to them because they understand that sometimes being still while the water moves is the most important thing you can do for yourself."

I watch Jada's expression go from serious to wistful. "That's really beautiful. You might have to teach me how to do that—be still, that is."

Jada turns her chin to me with a gentle smile. "Absolutely. Slumber party once school ends for the summer?"

I grin at the invitation. "Really?"

Jada snickers. "Yes, really. You say it like you're shocked you would ever be invited to stay the night at a friend's house."

Before I can stop myself, the truth pours out of me. "Well, that *is* the first time I've been invited to spend the night at a friend's house."

Jada's jaw drops, and instantly, I regret my honesty. "Are you serious? You've never had a sleepover?"

I shake my head, shrinking in my seat. "Nope. I wasn't exactly the popular girl. I was the shy girl with her nose in a book, most of the time afraid of her own voice. When you add bisexual to the mix, a lot of the girls didn't want me around."

Jada's hand goes over her heart. "Well, then we're going to do it up right. Facials, painting our nails, popcorn. We'll eat cookie dough until we barf. We have to watch a scary movie. Those are always best on my houseboat, where you're away from solid ground. We have to play truth or dare. I mean, you've missed out on all the classic moments. We've got a lot of ground to cover." She chucks my shoulder with affection. "Don't worry. Once school lets out for the year, I'll get you caught up."

I chuckle at her determination that I will somehow be normal. I won't drown in my own introversion that naturally shies away from new people and experiences.

But I'm not the girl I've always been. I'm not going to business school anymore. I'm not living in my parents' house. I'm not hiding from the world in my crappy apartment. I'm wild. I moved across the country to live with my aunt and start a new chapter.

I have two dogs now.

I can do this.

I grin at Jada, grateful for the beauty and daring she has brought into my life. She makes me feel new when I was certain I would never turn the next page to become a person I enjoyed being.

"Thank you," I tell her from the bottom of my heart. "I can't believe I get to go to a slumber party. That is the best idea, and the perfect remedy to his awful debacle with the murder weapon and Hank's hat showing up in the backyard. Thank you."

Jada nods her head once to signify that it's a done deal. "What are best friends for? Bring the dogs, bring your pajamas, and bring an iron stomach."

I love everything about this. "Will do."

Jada glances around. "Speaking of which, where is

Honey? I only see Cricket, who looks like she's trying to move into the space underneath your chair."

At mention of her name, Cricket scrambles out from under me and yips twice.

I reach down and pet her, my brows furrowing. "Where's your sister, Crick?" I stand, moving into the living room, where I assume Honey might be sleeping.

But Honey isn't there.

I frown, moving down the hallway. "Honey? Honey, come here, girl. Did you get shut inside a bedroom?" I check each room but see no sign of the bashful corgi.

Jada follows me into my bedroom, looking under my bed to make sure Honey isn't hiding there. "She's not here, Hannah."

Queasiness rushes through me at the prospect of having lost my dog the very week she has become mine on paper. "Are you serious? Honey!" I shout, horrified at the sound of nothing greeting me. "Honey, where are you?"

Jada stands, holding out her hand expectantly. "Here. Let me take your car around the block. Maybe she got out somehow and went for a run. She's still new to living here. It's possible she got out and couldn't find her way home."

I nod, my fingers numb from shock. "I don't under-stand. I didn't let her out. Aunt Em came from Phyllis' house to the station, so it wasn't her."

Jada shrugs after I toss her my keys. "Maybe Niles acci-dentally let her out when he was here? It's possible. I'll ask him about it while I'm out looking." She holds up her hands to me. "You stay here. Deputy Hanson is coming to deal with the hat situation. One of us has to be at the house. I'll go looking for Honey." Then she throws her arms around me. "We'll find her, Hannah. She can't have gotten far."

Pressure builds behind my eyes. "I'm a terrible dog mom!"

"No, you're not. We'll find her." Then Jada dashes out the door, taking my keys so she can snap into action, while I stand in the house like a dolt. I am hapless and unsure how any of this could possibly lead to a happy ending.

My stomach roils while I sit on the couch, my mind skipping as I try to retrace my steps to uncover where it all went wrong. I grind my fist into my temple, my lower lip quivering because my dog is missing. I can't even bring myself to work on the puzzle that rests on the coffee table beside my novel about innocent prairie romance.

Cricket hops up on the couch beside me, her maw tucking itself under my elbow because she can see I am falling apart.

Not two minutes pass before the backdoor opens and footsteps creak through the house.

I don't have the heart to call out to Aunt Em and ask how her interrogation went. I am completely hollow inside.

It's odd how attached to Honey I've become in such a short time. But just like Cricket, when Honey came into my life, she took up a permanent residence in my heart.

Cricket barks over and over, going from me to the back-door, alerting me to the fact that Aunt Em is in the house, and I should know about it.

Still, I don't get up or speak. I'm not sure I can.

My phone lights up with a text from Jada.

"NILES SAID WALLY STOPPED BY THE HOUSE WHILE HE WAS cleaning up the yard. Wally said he left his clipboard there."

MY BROWS KNIT IN CONFUSION. WALLY TOOK HIS CLIPBOARD with him to his truck. I saw him go with it.

Jada's next text comes through just as the pistons begin firing in my brain.

"HANNAH, I THINK WALLY IS TRYING TO FRAME YOU FOR HANK'S murder. He was the only other person in the backyard while we were gone."

THE TREAD COMES INTO THE KITCHEN, STILL OUT OF VIEW from where I sit on the couch. I want to greet my aunt, but I am too upset, too stunned to move.

Usually, my aunt would call for me, or I would hear her coo at Cricket, but when Cricket barks louder, I startle when a man's voice hits my ears. "Shut up, you stupid mutt, or I'll have to deal with you, too."

Ice hits my spine, stiffening my body where I sit on the couch. My sadness is pushed to the back of my mind while Cricket barks at the intruder who is clearly not welcome here. While I am still new to the area, at no point has a man ever let himself in through the backdoor of Aunt Em's home.

I open my mouth to call out, but my voice has deserted me. I pray hard for Deputy Hanson to get here quick, but part of me knows my luck isn't solid enough to be able to depend on a mercy like that.

I stand from the couch, my body moving slowly as my rubbery legs assure me that they've got this.

I hear rummaging in the kitchen, and Cricket barking with a menace that is not often heard on my happy-go-lucky Pomeranian.

"Get lost, you hear? I'll be in and out," he says to Cricket. "I'm putting this here, and then I'm going to call in an anonymous tip. They're going to take away the new girl, and then Larry will really be sorry he didn't give me that raise."

I balk at the logic the moment I confirm my suspicions by matching them with the voice that's intruded into my aunt's home.

My feet carry me into the kitchen, but the second I lay eyes on Wally, I know I've done the wrong thing. I should have run out the front door, away from the trespasser. I should have called the police again to tell them to hurry over.

I should have done anything but confront the man who came in through the backdoor to place a bloody bandana on the counter of the kitchen.

When I come face to face with Hank's killer, I know there's no going back now.

FRAMED

"Wally?" I rasp the moment my voice finds me. "You killed Hank!"

The guy who quoted me for lawncare this morning narrows his eyes at me, taking in my presence with a calculation I don't like one bit. "I saw your car leave," he says by way of accusation, as if I should have to justify why I am standing in the house where I reside.

"Where is Honey?" I holler at him, surprised at my own volume. Apparently, I can't speak up for myself, but if my dog's safety is in jeopardy, I can get all kinds of vocal. "Give me back my dog!"

Wally runs his fingers over his nose with a sneer. "That dog is going to die in Larry's backyard, so the cops can see he's an awful person. Then they're going to see that you killed Hank, now that there's plenty of evidence pointed your way. Larry will lose his favorite employee and his stellar reputation. He'll be known as a dog killer."

I balk at him. "Why did you kill Hank?" I ask, moving my back to the refrigerator and inching toward the block of knives on the counter. It's not much of a plan, but it's better than nothing. "What did Hank ever do to you?"

"I got fired because of him!" Wally shouts. "Hank complained to Larry that he couldn't find the mustard. Apparently, it was *my* job to keep the entire store perfectly stocked at all times with no help. Anytime something was missing, I took the heat for it. Well, I was tired of it!"

I startle at his shouting, my pulse spiking at the menace in his tone. My back glues itself to the counter as I inch toward the knives, so I have something with which to defend myself.

Now that Wally has told me his nefarious plan, I highly doubt he will let me go.

Wally motions wildly with his hands. "Hank's body in Larry's store? That should have been all the cops needed. But no. Who knew that the po-dunk police here wouldn't be easy to fool?" He points at me. "I've got nothing against you, new girl, other than the fact that you took my old job. Everyone is acting like you wear a halo, what with how they talk about how good you are at stocking shelves, as if it's an artform. Give me a break!"

Cricket sticks close to me, which gives me the courage to keep moving slowly toward the butcher block. "I didn't do anything to you, and you're trying to frame me. The knife in the flower bed? That was you! The hat in the bird bath?"

Though I don't need the verbal confirmation, Wally gives it up willingly. "It's nothing personal. Larry shouldn't have fired me. Hank shouldn't have complained about me to Larry, not after taking me out on his boat and acting all friendly. If they hadn't dealt me a raw deal, I wouldn't be here, trying to redirect their karma."

My nose scrunches. "That's what you think you're doing? You murdered a man! You're trying to frame me, even though you just said you know I did nothing wrong. What's your karma like?"

Wally's face twists, but he produces no answer or apology.

I am inches away from being able to defend myself, but it seems Wally has run out of patience. His gaze connects with where I am aiming my trajectory. "Not so fast!" He lunges for the butcher block, knocking me out of the way before I can reach for a knife.

Cricket growls, barking to let the world know that she doesn't like it when I am thrown around.

Wally yanks a knife free and aims it at me while I scramble to the far corner of the kitchen. "Run, Cricket!" I warn her, but my loyal Pomeranian doesn't have it in her to desert me when I am unarmed and unable to defend myself against all that threatens to tear me down.

Cricket leaps at Wally, but her slight frame is easy for him to kick aside with his sturdy boots.

Rage courses through me when Cricket yelps in pain. Fury the likes of which I don't often access rips through my bloodstream as Wally faces me with Aunt Em's purple steak knife clutched tight in his grip.

I don't need a knife. I don't need the backup of Deputy Hanson, who seems to be taking his sweet time getting here.

I don't need anything but sheer force of will when my dog's safety is at risk.

I rock forward and lunge at Wally, tackling him around the middle so hard that his body bangs against the counter, forcing an "oof!" sound from him.

He shoves me with vehemence, propelling me backward so he can brandish the knife between us to keep me at bay.

It's as if he thinks I won't go up against a knife if my dog is in danger.

Oh, how little he knows me.

Oh, how little I know myself, because reason deserts me, along with any sense of introversion or fear that might stunt my resolve. "You stole my dog," I growl at him, my upper lip curled.

Wally holds the knife between us, regarding my unexpected feral nature with wariness. "It's just a dog."

At this, something in me snaps. I throw my body at Wally, punching, slapping, and kicking with all my might. I will not let him take Honey from me so he can kill her and frame Larry. I will find my dog and rescue her if it's the last thing I do.

Which it very well might be.

I don't let up when the front door opens, and a rush of footsteps come for me. My fist doesn't know how to fight, but everything in me is willing to learn on the fly if it gets me one step closer to rescuing Honey. "Where is she?" I shout. "Give me back my dog!"

The knife slices hot across my right forearm, coaxing a scream from my lips while Cricket howls for my plight.

Still, I don't fall back. I will not surrender while Honey is out there, scared and lost.

She needs me. Hank died, leaving her afraid and alone. She's a meek soul and needs someone who will fight for her safety when she is too wary of using her voice to make her presence known.

Honey and I are the same. We need each other.

Though I have nothing in me but desperation and love for my dogs, my fist aims itself without pulling back, connecting with Wally's jaw so hard that my knuckles smart at the contact.

Deputy Hanson charges into the kitchen, his weapon drawn as he shoves Wally to the side so I can escape. In a move so seamless, I can scarcely understand how the dance begins and ends, the deputy whirls Wally around, slamming his wrist to the edge of the counter until the knife clatters onto the kitchen floor.

I back away from the scene as blood slides down my

arm and drips off my wrist. My breath comes in stuttering gasps while I try unsuccessfully to steady myself through the waves of horror. "Honey!" I call out after the deputy finishes reading Wally his rights. "Where is Honey?"

The officer jerks Wally to stand straight, facing me so he can see my distress. "You stole her dog? It wasn't enough to kill Hank? You had to go after his dog, too?"

Wally's upper lip curls. "The stupid dog is in my truck."

That's all the information I need. I don't care why Wally did it, or what his grand plans were for Larry's demise. I care about Honey, who has been through enough.

I race out of the house with Cricket by my side, tripping over my own two feet. I run to Wally's lawncare truck and throw open the door. "Honey? Honey!"

The moment my sweet corgi licks my face, relief hits me so hard; I stagger to the side. Tears slide down my cheeks with no end in sight.

"I'm so sorry! I didn't know Wally would come for you. You tried to warn me! Honey, I'll never leave you alone again!"

I pull my short-legged friend from the truck and sit down in the middle of the street so I can wrap my arms around both my dogs, accidentally smearing my blood onto their fur. My heart swells at the love that comes freely and easily. I can tell neither of them blame me for dropping the ball on keeping them safe from Wally and his evil designs. They don't care about any of it.

Over and over, they lick my face, barking while they try to tell me all the things I didn't listen to before.

I didn't realize that Honey's growl at Wally meant something. "You were trying to tell me, weren't you! You recognized Wally and you wanted him out of our lives. You growled at him, telling me that he was unsafe." I hold Honey tighter while Cricket licks us both. "You had to be in the same space with the guy who murdered Hank! You poor thing!"

I am beside myself, so much that I don't even notice Jada pulling up until she runs to me and kneels beside us. Aunt Em is close behind, tears streaming from her cheeks to match mine.

The two women hem us in with a hug that garners them plenty of dog kisses.

I sag in their embrace, sobbing through my relief that Honey is finally safe. Hank's killer will be behind bars, where he belongs.

27

HANK'S WILL

Turning in a completed puzzle is bittersweet. After spending so much time and concentration putting a beautiful nature scene together, it's hard to break apart all the pieces and march the box back to Puzzles and Pins. I love the Puzzle Exchange Program, and have my sights set on a new one that I can't wait to dive into.

With my dogs by my side, I browse through the lengthy selection on the long wall in the store, chatting with Vivian about the ups and downs of owning a storefront in a town that is largely tourist based.

"This one," I finally rule, stopping in front of a puzzle that is only five hundred pieces. "I need an easy win. It's been a long week."

Vivian wraps her arm around my shoulders and gives me a quick side-squeeze. "I heard about Wally. Just awful.

To think anyone could be so cruel as to kill a man like Hank in cold blood, and then add dognapping to it all?" She shakes her head. "I'm grateful you got out of there. The entire town is grateful Honey is safe. She's been through a lot." She smirks at the dogs who rarely leave my side. "In fact," she says, digging into her apron. She pulls out two dog treats, holding them aloft until Cricket and Honey both sit at attention for her. "I was saving two special treats for these soul sisters. They're the last from the bacon flavored bag."

She leans down to scratch the girls behind their ears while I slide a detailed closeup puzzle of a squirrel from the shelf.

"This town is good at being gentle to Honey. She gets all the love she needs from everyone we pass." I am about to ask Vivian how often she gets new puzzles in, but my phone rings, so I pull it from my pocket and answer it, since I've been expecting a call from Jada on her lunch break.

There is a kindergartener in her class who draws pictures of all the dogs in the town. I've been hoping he'll do one of Honey. Jada swore she would call me the moment it happened.

"Did Anthony finally draw a picture of Honey?" I ask in lieu of a greeting.

The male voice on the other end confuses me enough that I check my screen. "Hello? This is Javier Rodriquez. Is this Hannah Hart?"

My shoulders relax as the number I kept not answering these past couple of days suddenly makes sense. "Oh! Hi, Javier. Yes, this is Hannah. Is everything okay with Honey's adoption? Did I forget to sign something important?"

He sounds relieved to have connected with me. "No. Well, sort of. Can you stop by my office? Preferably today, if you can. It's about Honey."

My stomach knots. As if she can sense my unease, Honey inches closer to my side. "Sure. Is everything okay?" I shouldn't have ignored those calls. I rarely answer numbers I don't recognize, but being that I'm new in town, I probably shouldn't stick too close to that general rule of thumb.

"Yes, just a few more loose ends to tie up."

I swallow hard, worried that Javier may have learned that Honey was dognapped under my care. Will he want to have Honey taken from me?

"I'll be there soon, then. On my way to you." I end the call, nervous that something may have come up that might take Honey away. I love her so much. I can't imagine my life without her. Cricket needs her.

I need her.

I check out the squirrel puzzle and walk home with the dogs, so I can drive us to the law office, where I sincerely hope nothing bad is awaiting our arrival.

Honey knows I am upset, so she sticks close to me.

Cricket is her usual goofball self. She demands to sit

beside me in the passenger's seat so she can rest her head on my thigh while I drive.

I'm not sure that's the safest way to do things, but it works for us.

Cricket licks the bandage from where Wally sliced my right forearm with the kitchen knife. My dogs take such good care of me.

Honey pants on the floor of the passenger's side. She is not daring enough to hop onto the seat beside Cricket and gaze at the scenery whooshing by. They are both such beautiful dogs with the sweetest dispositions.

As I drive to the law office, I begin to work up a speech as to why I should be able to keep Honey, despite whatever problem there is with her paperwork.

By the time I get there, my hand is clammy, but I am no less determined to make a case that my dog needs to stay with me. I won't bottle up my feelings and nod along because there are more important adults in the room. I will make a firm stand and do all it takes to keep Honey with me.

After fist-fighting Wally to rescue Honey from his clutches, I am less inclined to crawl into my shell when my dog needs me.

I take out the leashes and attach them to their collars, kissing both dogs because I cannot resist their sweet faces.

My voice is mousy when I greet the receptionist, who sends us back to Javier's office.

The door is cracked open, so I wave to him before

letting myself into his space. "Hi. I came as soon as I could." Before Javier can even open his mouth to greet me, I hold up my hand. "Before you say anything that might mean that Honey can't stay with me, let me just say that I love this dog. She belongs in Apple Blossom Bay. She loves being with Cricket and with me. I will do whatever it takes to make sure she has a good life. I buy her the pricier food Hank gave her, so she doesn't get an upset tummy. I walk her multiple times every day. She goes with me to work, so she's not alone all day long. Whatever the problem is with the adoption, please tell me how to fix it. I love Honey, and she does well with Cricket and me." I kneel so I can gather both my dogs to me, bracing myself in case someone is coming to take her away. "We belong together."

Javier's mouth curves into a knowing smile as he straightens his tie. "Then that makes what I have to tell you that much better. I don't often get to deliver good news to good people who deserve a little sunshine. Or, in your case, a whole heap of sunshine." He opens a folder and pulls out an official-looking form. "This is the last will and testament of Hank. He was very specific how his assets should be handled. I drew up his will myself, so I can tell you for certain that this is what he wanted, so this is how it will be, no matter who disapproves."

I gnaw on my lower lip, preparing myself to see something horrible, like Honey being given to one of his children who don't even want her.

What will I do if that's the case? Can I really fight Hank's will?

"I can't look," I admit, turning my head away and burying my face in Honey's fur.

I can hear the smirk in Javier's voice. "I'll sum it up for you, then. Hank loved Honey more than anything. He wanted to make sure she was cared for if she outlived him. He set aside money in an account that is to be used solely for the care and upkeep of Honey."

My nose crinkles. "What?"

"That money will be given to you, so you can feed and care for Honey without breaking your bank."

I slowly turn my head to the lawyer, my mouth falling open as I try to piece together his words. "But that... That's not bad news. Right? I'm hearing you say that Honey's food is going to be paid for?"

Javier nods, clearly amused at my confusion. "It's very good news, but that's not all."

I gape at him, stilling all movement, lest I breathe too hard and the whole thing tumble like a poorly constructed house of cards. "What?"

Javier flips to a new page, which is accompanied by a pink slip of paper and several official looking documents. "The thing Hank loved second-most was his boat. He used to take Honey out in it all the time. He worried that when he was gone, Honey would miss being out on the water. So, Hank willed the boat to the person who agreed to take Honey in. But he told me very specifically not to let that information slip until someone took Honey in just because they loved her, and not because they wanted his money or his boat."

I blink at the lawyer, certain I heard him wrong. I don't speak for several seconds, so Javier repeats himself, giving me the same information slightly reworded.

When that doesn't sink in all the way, he comes out from behind his desk and shows me line by line that yes, Hank wanted Honey provided for financially. She's ten years old, which means more trips to the vet. Plus, her food is running me more than a hundred dollars a month, which is no small expense.

But the boat?

I gape at Javier, and finally my voice finds me. "I've never heard of a person willing their boat to their dog's new owner. Is that even legal?"

I don't know why I'm arguing myself out of something amazing happening, but I can't seem to stop myself.

Javier kneels and runs his fingers over Honey's fur. "Hank loved Honey very much. I think it would do his heart good to look down on his dog and know she is taken care of. You're providing the love and care, and Hank is funding the rest. His will stipulates that his money should also be used to pay the boat slip."

My lower lip quivers because I am filled to the brim with emotion that is threatening to start leaking from my tear ducts. "But I don't know how to swim! And Hank's children wanted his boat so badly."

Javier shrugs without an ounce of visible sympathy for Hank's bickering children. "I guess they'll have to fight over his house, then. That'll keep them good and miserable. This will is ironclad, so it's a done deal." Javier stands, taking a set of two keys from his top drawer. "Hannah Hart, you might want to invest in swim lessons. Hank's boat is officially yours." He leans in conspiratorially. "And if you even so much as think about giving the boat to Hank's children, I will have you committed for such an insane idea. They are horrible people, and this was Hank's choice. They'll respect it, and so will you." Javier drops the keys to the boat into my palm and closes my fingers around them.

I don't understand how such luck found me here, out of all the out of the way places, but when I look up at Javier while he helps me sign the necessary paperwork, I realize that I might have to get used to the fact that life is peppered with enough beautiful moments to get me through.

All I have to do is enjoy the sunshine and snuggle my dogs. Thanks to Hank's love of Honey, that just might be possible for me.

28

STOLEN SOUND SYSTEM CELEBRATION

"Are you sure this is safe?" I yell to Aunt Em, who is dancing in her clown suit on the sand a few feet from me. While she normally does balloon animals for the kids, it is too windy for that tonight, so she is entertaining her adoring fans with a silly dance.

Aunt Em blows a raspberry in my direction. "Safe? Who said anything about safe? It's fun, my little grapefruit. It's nothing but fun."

I grumble under my breath that silly concepts like safety keep me alive while I enjoy the fun, but that doesn't seem to be the proper sentiment of the evening.

I've never been to a bonfire of this magnitude before. The sound system Jada and I stole plays Dolly Parton's greatest hits because that is what Aunt Em, Edna, Phyllis and Dorothy insisted should be blasted out across the water.

When Deputy Hanson commented on the sound system half an hour ago, Aunt Em answered him with a merry, "Isn't it great? We stole it from City Hall!"

Deputy Hanson laughed, of all things, clutching a tall cup of lemonade, clad in an undershirt, cut-offs, and bare feet.

I do not understand this town.

It's like the whole of Apple Blossom Bay has decided to come out and celebrate, though I have no idea what the occasion is that warrants such unfettered jubilee. There are pockets of praise for Hank and plenty of cups lifted to toast his memory. Perhaps this is to serve as a wake of some sort, so the town can celebrate a life lived well.

All I know is that my feet have been strapped into skis while the water laps over my legs, and I regret this choice very much. "I think I mentioned that I don't know how to swim," I remind my aunt loud enough that Phyllis, Edna, and Dorothy can hear me from inside Hank's boat.

Phyllis calls over her shoulder to me while my aunt dances to the music booming out of the sound system Jada and I stole. "That's why you're wearing a life jacket," Phyllis explains from the helm of Hank's boat.

I mean, technically, it's *my* boat now, but I don't know the first thing about it. People have been congratulating me all day on my good fortune, but my only response has been to insist that I didn't know this was coming, assuming they think I must have had nefarious motives when I offered to take Honey in.

My dogs are playing with sticks on the shore, which the children on the beach throw over and over in a never-ending game of fetch.

My fingers shake on the bar. My right arm winds through to keep the bar tight in my queasy grip while Hank's boat slowly pulls me toward the open water.

I can hear Jada shrieking behind me, cheering me on from the shore because she is proud of me for taking a risk this big. Her brother is beside her to my right, sipping his lemonade in the glow of the bonfire while he smirks at the mess I've gotten myself into.

Niles knows I don't know how to swim.

I'm about to drown right in front of my crush and my best friend, all while they cheer on my impending death.

I don't know the first thing about owning a boat, but Aunt Em insisted I should get out on it first thing. Hank's boat, apparently, is a very nice boat, which everyone keeps commenting on.

To me, they all look similar. It's got an engine, a few seats and an awning or something over the back half. Other than that, I'm out as far as cataloging the details.

My stomach is in my throat because when I insisted I was too nervous to attempt driving the boat, it was decided that Phyllis would take the wheel while Aunt Em slapped water skis and a life jacket on me.

"Let's go, Hannah!" Phyllis cheers while Edna gives me a thumbs up.

"Wait, I changed my mind!" I shout to her, but the engine purrs too loudly for her to hear my protest.

That, or Phyllis isn't about to let me chicken out.

I could let go of the bar. I could sit my butt back in the shallow water and announce to the world that I might never be ready to try new things.

But that's just it. I might never be ready, so it stands to reason that there is no sense in waiting for the right time or the perfect setting.

The opportunity to go waterskiing is now, so I grip the bar with all my might. A scream rips out of me as my body moves through the water under the moonlight. The sleek, black vessel takes me farther than I could stand and still be able to keep my head above water.

My scream is mingled with excitement. It sounds much like a crazed bird squawking at top volume. I can't hear or see anything but the boat and the water.

I can't think about the water. I don't want to dwell on how easy it would be for me to drown. Edna isn't exactly going to jump in and save me. She's hooting and hollering her joy, assuming my screams of fright are a jolly celebration.

Dorothy, on the other hand, can see my anxiety from where she sits on the boat near Phyllis. I can tell she has no intention of letting me chicken out, judging by the wicked grin widening her thin face.

It's now or never.

I grip the bar as the boat pulls me to standing.

And suddenly, I am skiing. Though I have no idea how I am mastering the feat, it seems all I have to do is keep my legs from folding and hold on tight.

I can do that. I held onto the idea that I could track down Hank's killer.

I held onto the notion that I needed to adopt Honey, despite any complications.

I can hold onto this bar.

At least, that's what I tell myself as I race across the water's surface on the skis, shrieking my terror as Jada, Niles, Aunt Em and the bulk of the residents of Apple Blossom Bay cheer me on from the shore.

The breeze slices across my face, drying my wide eyes and swallowing my shrieks of terror.

It feels like an hour that I am hanging on for dear life, or maybe it's only been a handful of minutes. But when the boat finally slows, my body flops into the water. My limbs don't know what to do with themselves, so they panic and chop at the waves, holding tight to the bar at the end of the slacked rope. I have no solid rhythm to my movements or plan in my head. Aunt Em talked me over how to ski, not how to stay alive after the boat came to a stop.

Jada races to the dock, shouting commands over her giggles, but it's Niles who lowers himself into the idling boat beside Phyllis and reels in the rope I haven't let go of yet.

I don't know how he manages it, but Niles somehow brings me into the boat while chuckling at my fright.

"What did you think was going to happen? You're wearing a life vest. You weren't going to drown."

I shiver in the back of the boat while Phyllis, Edna, and Dorothy comment on the smooth ride. I sit on the side seat while I try unsuccessfully to remove my feet from the skis. "I did it," I breathe, adrenaline rushing through me.

Niles kneels to help free my rubbery legs from the skis. His hands on my ankles are the only warm spot on my body. "You did it!" he says, looking up at me with a smile. "After the month you've had, I'm not sure there's anything you can't do."

I pray the moonlight conceals the worst of my blush.

Pride rushes through my veins, straightening my spine while Edna helps Phyllis dock the boat.

My best friend jumps into the vessel and throws her arms around me the second it's secured in place. Suddenly, I am warm where I need it most. "You were amazing! You're a real boat owner now."

My dogs bark at me from the shore, simultaneously proud of me and cautious of my daring.

I laugh at myself, unsure how I got to this point in my life where I could jump into the unknown and face my fears.

"I think it's official," Jada rules.

"What?" I ask, leaning into her hug while Niles takes the spot on my other side.

Jada grins at me, motioning to the open water. "You belong here."

And just like that, I realize that Jada is right. I do belong in Apple Blossom Bay with the people I love, whether or not I can swim.

The End.
Love the book?
Leave a review!

BULLDOG BANDIT

Inheriting a fancy boat is a privilege I didn't not anticipate finding its way to me. Not only do I know nothing about running the sleek motorized vessel, but I also cannot swim—a fact my Aunt Emily assured me is a mere technicality.

Can people learn to swim when they were born with symbrachydactyly? Absolutely. Being born without my right hand hasn't slowed me down in life. It's more that drowning terrifies me, and I don't have fantastic coordination to begin with.

Plus, the man who volunteered to teach me to swim is Jada's older brother. It wouldn't be so problematic to have Niles Williams teach me to swim if he wasn't the handsomest man in the world. But being that I've nearly drowned twice in his presence since I've met him, I'm grateful that Edna is going to teach me how to swim this evening.

I love summertime in general but living in Apple Blossom Bay makes everything smell fresher and look that much more vibrant. Nature is exploding everywhere I look. There are trees flowering in all colors as I walk with my two dogs to the beach not half a mile from where I now live with my quirky Aunt Em.

After my shift spent working at the Forgotten Stock Market where I keep the groceries for the town perfectly aligned on the shelves, I went home and retrieved my bathing suit, which hasn't been worn in several years.

I think I heard the thing whimper when I took it out of my drawer.

With jean cutoffs and a tank top over my bathing suit, I should be ready for an evening at the beach with Edna— my sweet friend in her seventies who breaks me out of my shell from time to time.

Do I feel silly asking for swimming lessons as a twenty-five-year-old woman?

Yes.

But I've decided I don't care if I make a fool of myself in front of Edna if it keeps me from drowning.

I stop halfway to the beach, pausing to give my toy Pomeranian and my squat corgi some water from a portable dish. "Oh, Cricket. We can take a break. You're panting so hard."

I run my fingers over her thick red-brown-blonde fur coat as I kiss the top her of her head. Cricket was the first dog that found me when I moved to Apple Blossom Bay, and my life has never been the same.

The second dream come true is Honey—the caramel-colored corgi I took in when her owner, Hank, lost his life and couldn't provide a home for Honey any longer. With the adoption of Honey came the deed to Hank's boat, which I still have not grown the confidence to take for a spin.

First things first: I need to learn to swim.

Then I can learn to drive a boat.

Or, more likely, Jada can drive the boat while I cling to the thing for dear life.

I rub the silk of Honey's ear between my fingers. "Are you ready to see Mommy try to swim? I'm guessing you'll do laps around me."

Honey yips in reply, then goes back to rubbing her nose in the sand so long as my hand is on her.

Gotta love a dog who's just as dependent on me as I am on her. My introversion takes a backseat whenever I have my dogs with me.

The walk to the beach is short and sunny, though I wish it was longer, being that when I get there, I am going to have to get in the water and practice not drowning.

I remove my flip-flops when I get onto the sand, walking toward the water's edge where Edna is standing in a bright yellow bikini. My friend is wearing the sunniest smile I've seen all day. "Hey, stranger!" she calls to me, flagging me over in case the bright yellow of her suit didn't alert me to her location. The people of Apple Blossom Bay don't let good weather go to waste. There are several families with giant parasols scattered along the beach, huge sandcastles with moats, and children splashing in the ocean. Edna is chatting with a woman who looks like she was born with a permanent scowl.

It's going to be fine. I can do this.

I hug Edna when I reach her, because that is also a very Apple Blossom Bay thing to do. Everyone is jolly with affection here, which never appealed to me back when I lived in Chicago. But now that I'm here, I find I don't mind the lavish nature of their affection one bit.

"Thanks for this, Edna. Really. If you hadn't forced me here, I wouldn't even try."

"Try what?" the woman beside Edna asks. She flicks back a gray curl from her rounded face.

"Swimming," I admit. "I don't know how to swim, so Edna was gracious enough to offer me a lesson."

The woman scoffs. "I'm Gertrude. You're Emily's niece. The new girl. Hannah. You took Hank's boat, yet you don't know how to swim?"

I swallow hard at the irony with which I still have not been able to make peace. "I inherited Hank's boat, yes."

Gertrude eyes me as if I showed up to a formal dinner with a squid atop my head. "Utter waste. That boat's a beauty. You should sell it to me. I'd give you a fair price."

I wasn't expecting to confront anyone other than the waves this morning, so I scramble for the right words. "Out of respect for Hank, I'm going to keep the boat. He wanted it to be used to take Honey out on the ocean, so I'm going to learn how to do that."

The woman grumbles several unfriendly half-sentences in response.

Edna motions to her friend with a hint of impatience on her usually cheery face. "Have you met Gertrude? She goes for morning walks on the beach sometimes, spreading her sunshine wherever she goes."

I offer my hand for her to shake, but she sniffs at me and turns, walking away across the sand.

My stomach drops. "Maybe this wasn't a good idea. Gertrude is right. I have no right owning a boat like Hank's. I don't even know how to swim!"

Edna beams at me, her bony arms squeezing me tight before she pulls back to get a good look at me. "We're going to have fun, alright? It's not as scary as you're thinking. Ignore Gertrude. She's always bent out of shape about something."

I keep my expression light even as the panicked truth spills out of me in a gust. "We're going to have fun out there? Really? Because my nightmares last night were torn between me drowning, and me being eaten by a shark, then drowning."

Edna chuckles at my anxiety. "Eaten by a shark? That hardly ever happens."

I balk at her, screeching a scared, "What?"

Edna pats my back, motioning to the water. "Let's get in. The waves will do the rest."

Easy for her to say. The ocean is Edna's happy place. It makes her come alive when she's down and clears her mind when she needs a meditative moment.

There are several boats out on the water, far away from the spots marked for swimming. "There are more boats today than usual," I comment. "Any reason?"

Edna motions to a sign tacked to a post on the dock. "The annual local fishing competition is coming up. They're all out there practicing. Testing out different baits in different spots of the ocean to see what gives them the best return." Edna walks out into the water without pause, confident in her awesomeness that nothing will ever be too hard for her.

I wish I had that belief. Some days, every little thing feels too big for me to tackle. Though, since I adopted Honey and Cricket, those days have been decidedly fewer.

I unhook their leashes from the carabiner on my belt loop, letting them run free so they can be as wild as they like. They're well-behaved dogs, and the children of Apple Blossom Bay adore Cricket. Honey is far more reserved, shying away from most people who are not me, but Cricket's sweet nature gives her the confidence to try new things —just like Cricket's gregarious smile does for me.

And now I'm here, about to try something I have failed at every time I've attempted it.

My tank top and shorts drop to the sand beside the

towel I've had tucked under my arm. I should probably get a new, nicer swimsuit, but this drab pale green one from high school is probably fine.

That's the theory, anyway, until I take a step forward and realize that the material is too tight and is wedged firmly between my cheeks.

That's more motivation to get into the water, so I can dig the bathing suit out, in hopes it never does that again.

This is already starting out poorly.

Edna rests her hands on the water's surface as she peers to her left. "Hannah, who did you lend your boat to?"

My nose crinkles as I step into the water, cringing at how cold it is on my ankles. "No one. It's docked in the spot where it's always been, right…" But when I turn to the spot where Hank's boat should be on the other side of the pier, my mouth falls open when the spot is vacant. "That's where it's supposed to be, right? Did I get turned around?"

There are so many boats; perhaps I'm just not seeing it. I still can't believe it's mine, so it's an afterthought when I'm at the beach.

Edna frowns as she points in the distance. "That's your boat way out there. Hank's was always the only black boat. Did you forget to tie it to the dock? It doesn't look like it's driving, just drifting with the waves."

A panicked squeal sticks in my throat. "How do we get it back? And no, I didn't forget to tie it up. I haven't untied it at all! I don't know how to drive the thing, so the most

I've done is sit on it, and that was with you, Phyllis, Dorothy, and Aunt Em yesterday."

Edna grimaces. "Swimming lessons will have to be postponed today." She flags down a man I recognize as being one of Hank's poker buddies, who is an avid fisher. "Dave, we need your boat!" she calls.

I get out of the water, thankful to have escaped swimming lessons as I tug on my jean shorts. "Hank's boat is floating out there. Did you see anyone on it?" I ask as I trot toward him on the dock. It looks like he just came back from an afternoon of fishing. I can tell by his expression that he would very much like to go home with his kill. But to his credit, Dave bobs his head and motions for us to follow him onto Erma's Heart—his boat which he just docked.

The white vessel is nice with a tinge of a fishy stink to it, which I'm guessing is a good thing if the purpose was to practice for the fishing competition.

Cricket and Honey are displeased to see me putting distance between myself and them, but I promise them I'll return soon. I worry the two might jump into the water to follow me, but to their credit, they go back to playing with the children on the shore. Though, I can feel them watching me as Dave wipes his fishy hands on his cargo shorts and restarts the motor to his boat.

Edna sees no need for shorts or a coverup, but wears her yellow bikini with pride, owning her body without apology.

Why can't I do that?

Dave takes us out to my boat, cutting the engine for the moment so he can call to whomever is on my boat that most definitely shouldn't be. I don't so much care that someone stole my boat; I care that someone thought Hank's boat would be up for a joyride, thus disrespecting his memory.

When no one answers the call, Dave secures his boat to Hank's with a rope in a move so deft, I scarcely understand how it happened. He secures the lasso over the hook on the front of the boat and anchors it to Erma's Heart. "If no one's on that boat, could be that it wasn't tied securely to the dock, and it just drifted out to sea. Lucky you spotted it when you did, I guess. The waves aren't too active today, so it's probably been drifting for a while if it got this far."

Dave lectures me on boat safety, but I'm not really listening. I have no plans to ever take Hank's boat out on my own, so I don't need to learn the details just yet.

Dave's boat moves slowly through the waters, so as not to cause Hank's vessel to knock into his on the trek back. Though I've been on my boat a handful of times since I inherited it, the movements are still unfamiliar to me as Dave motors us to the dock. He parks Erma's Heart and then jumps out, doing me a favor by bringing Hank's boat beside his to the dock. "You'll have to park it properly in a minute, but for now, this'll do. The person who owns the spot next to mine will be out on the water for a while, so there's not a huge rush. But each spot belongs to a designate person, so I'll help you move it once we see what's what."

I turn to Dave, confused. "I thought you said it's likely the boat just got loose and drifted off to sea. What other explanation could there be?"

"Pirates," Edna supplies with a mischievous look to her petite and wiry features.

It's not until Dave has both vessels secured to the dock that I venture onto Hank's boat. It's sleek and bigger than the others. I am completely undeserving of the gift that came with the adoption of Honey. I can hear my corgi barking from the shore, letting me know that she did not enjoy our short time spent apart.

My head tilts to the side when I realize that Honey's barks are joined by a second dog, which sounds far closer to me than the shore.

I survey the sand for Cricket, catching her playing with a woman, jumping back and forth like a grasshopper for her amusement.

What a little ham.

The second bark isn't coming from any dog I can place. My brows crinkle as I move onto the dock from Erma's Heart and then step into my black boat, noting the difference a larger vessel makes as far as standing steadier in the water with fewer interruptions from the waves.

As I walk on the deck, the canine whine gets louder, quickening my steps along with my heart rate.

My hand goes over my mouth to stifle a squeal when I

see a sweet little gray English bulldog wagging his curled little tail and panting at me. "Oh, a stowaway!"

Edna gasps at the sight, her hands pressed over her heart. "Who is that? Is this our pirate?"

I chuckle as I kneel, giving the dog a healthy two feet of space, in case he or she doesn't prefer strangers. "Hi, sweetheart. Are you a pirate? Did you make off with my boat?" I tease the dog who is a little smaller than Honey, but larger than Cricket.

I open my mouth to ask another sing-song question, but Edna's scream stiffens my spine. I whirl around to decipher the source of her worry, but see nothing of note near my friend. I follow her line of vision, angling my body forward to examine the source of her worry.

No words come out of my mouth when I see a bloody hand resting on a spot to the right of the dog on the deck.

I was supposed to learn how to swim today, but it looks like I'll be talking to the police instead.

Read *Bulldog Bandit* by Molly Maple today!

PEANUT BUTTER GINGER DOG
BISCUITS

Yield: 20 treats

Bentley crosses her arms and leans her hip on the side of the kiosk, gearing up to educate me. "Ceylon cinnamon is better for your liver than the regular ground stuff you find at the grocery store (which is usually cassia cinnamon). It's also a bit sweeter, so you don't have to use as much in the syrups to really make the flavor shine."

I absorb the new information, making a mental note to get Ceylon cinnamon the next time I go grocery shopping. My dogs deserve the best of the best in their treats.

-Corgi Crisis by Molly Maple

Ingredients for Biscuits:

2 1/3 cup almond flour
½ cup peanut butter
2 Tbsp ground ginger
1 Tbsp Ceylon cinnamon
1-2 Tbsp water, as needed

Instructions for Biscuits:

1. Preheat oven to 350 degrees F.
2. Using a stand mixer, combine the almond flour, peanut butter, ground ginger and Ceylon cinnamon, mixing until the dough is sticky and well combined.
3. If needed, add 1-2 Tbsp water.
4. Form dough into a large ball and then roll out on a nonstick surface until dough is ½ an inch thick.
5. Using a cookie cutter, cut out your cookies in whatever shape you like, and place them on a lined baking tray.
6. Bake 15-20 minutes.
7. Turn off the oven and leave the tray in the oven for 30 minutes.
8. Remove from oven and store in an airtight container for up to ten days.